Edward Everett Hale

My Friend, the Boss

A Story of today

Edward Everett Hale

My Friend, the Boss
A Story of today

ISBN/EAN: 9783744747578

Printed in Europe, USA, Canada, Australia, Japan

Cover: Foto ©Andreas Hilbeck / pixelio.de

More available books at **www.hansebooks.com**

MY FRIEND THE BOSS.

A Story of To-day.

BY

EDWARD E. HALE,

Author of "Hampton," "Mr. Tangier's Vacations," "Ten Times One is Ten," "In His Name," "A Man without a Country," Etc., Etc.

———oo°o°oo———

BOSTON:

J. STILMAN SMITH & COMPANY.

1888.

PREFACE.

IT is always interesting to see how rich men spend their money. It often seems as if they took more pleasure in earning it than in spending it. Sometimes it seems as if they did not know how to spend it when it was earned.

In the best days of Athens, and in some of the days which were not the best, the rich men of that city fairly vied with each other in showing how they could expend large sums in its public service. Happily for us, we see such people now, — as when a man spends largely to improve the music of a city, or a woman to improve its schools.

I have thought that a man might, with as much interest, spend his money in securing good government for his home, as in making sure that he had a good yacht, or in maintaining a fine stable of fast horses. Men spend money to secure their own election to public office. It would be more agreeable to spend money wisely, for making good government sure, without spoiling the expenditure by the taint of corruption.

"My Friend the Boss," as he says himself, likes good government, is willing to give his time to secure it, and, with his time, his money. He does this in a legitimate way, and he has his reward.

This little book was in type some years ago, but its publication has been deferred by a series of accidents.

EDWARD E. HALE.

Boston, July 8, 1888.

CONTENTS.

MY FRIEND .THE BOSS.

CHAPTER I.

THE train was exactly on time. We rolled into a cheerful and comfortable station, perfectly lighted by electricity, and, as I staggered from the car with bag, valise, shawl and umbrella all in my hands, it was into noonday light that I descended.

In a moment a natty groom took from me these impediments, almost without asking leave, and in a moment more I was shaking hands with his master.

"Know you?" said he, "I should think so! Saw you on the platform. There are not so many of your build, and really your hair has stood test better than most of us." So we walked to his comfortable carriage. My "traps" or "plunder" were put in, Michael went back with the check for my trunk, and John and I went on talking together, as we had done thirty years before, and as if we had not parted for a week.

In truth we had parted thirty years before, as I say, at the corner of Hollis, at half-past four in the morning. Our class supper had ended, perhaps half an hour before, and John and I had stood there, talking, in the early dawn. Street cars were just invented. He took the earliest car into town that he might catch such lightning express for the West as then existed. I went to bed. We shook hands heartily, and he said, "God knows when we shall meet again." Thirty years had sent us backward and forward over the world, in fun, and in fight, in good fortune and bad, and at last we met,—as I say, under the Arc-lights in the station house at Tamworth.

"When have you seen Gilman? And how is Flagg?" Such questions, and a world of others like them, crowded our little ride.

His house is a palace, and a large one at that. Many a courier in Europe has dragged me to see many a palace of this or that little King of Bavaria, or Würtemberg, or Weiss-nicht-Wo, in which no one would display such generous hospitality as could John in this house in Waban Avenue. On the other hand, the traditions of Waban, whoever he was, still held here, and one had here also, the homely comforts of a log cabin. There is but one other palace known to me, of which one can say the same. The family had dined, but after I had washed and dressed, my cheerful little din-ner was served, and John and his wife, and two or three wide-awake boys and girls, gave me moral support and com-fort, as I ate it. In fifteen minutes more I was as much at home with the children as if I had gone to chapel with them for four years, as I had with their father, and had, with them, prompted and been prompted through difficult passages in Æschines and Isocrates.

As eight o'clock drew near, it proved that some of them were going to the concert of the Jubal Club. Would I like to hear the music, or would I rest in the library?

"Tired!" I was not tired. How should I be tired after seven hours in that comfortable Wagner palace? I have been far more tired after three hours in my own study, with Tom, Dick and Harry; Miss A., Miss B. and Miss C.; Mrs. X., Mrs. Y. and Mrs. Z., all just "looking in for a moment," and " so sorry to interrupt me, and knowing how busy I was,—but would I just be kind enough to grind their dull axes for them ? " Now, in the Wagner, nobody calls on you, there is no mail, the telegram cannot find you, you have one or two good novels, and, if you want, you may write a chapter in your Serial, or a leader for the Daily Argus. You have everything except a dead grandfather and a hornet's nest to make you comfortable, and there is no man to terrify or make afraid.

I was not at all tired, and so I joined the Jubal party. Two carriages came to the door, and people appeared whom I had not seen. They were not then explained to me, but I came to know them well, and so will this reader, I hope.

The music was very good. But I believe I was more taken by the house and by the orchestra. I said to myself, for the hundredth time, that when, at the West, they do a thing, they do it with the finest edge and the most perfect polish. I had seen no such Opera House as this in Philadelphia or New York. Far less had I seen any such audience in Munich, or in Florence. Good-natured, easily pleased,—yes, that is the habit of people, in proportion as they are near a frontier. They have not yet got over the habit of thanking God that they have anything. They measure the concert against the howling wilderness still, and do not compare it with some reminiscence of what it was when Arion led the orchestra, and Orpheus was the tenor. But this was not merely the good-natured audience of Cheyenne or of Tombstone. I knew those audiences. These people knew what was good, and listened, and were still, and applauded sympathetically. Regarding which sympathy of theirs, I was to learn more.

" Tumble into any carriage," cried John to me, as I stood

under the great porte-cochère with his daughter Nelly, after all was over. "Do not stay on the order of your coming." And I dimly made out, that in place of the two carriages which had brought us, four or five were now receiving our party, and that the party, somehow, had grown. And, when we came back to Waban Avenue, this proved to be so. Into the large drawing-room,—come not the little home party only, but people whom I had not seen, and, among them, one or two whom I was quite sure that I had seen on the stage. A Mr. Ferguson, whose exquisite violin had brought back the Ole Bull of my boyhood, and Mrs. Savage, one of the soprano singers, with a voice which made you love her, rather than admire her. Sure enough, we had with us the very choicest of the musical authorities of the town.

We congratulated and we made our compliments. We sank into tête-à-tête chairs and talked gravely about Wagner, and gladly about Mozart. I was listening to a very curious story about something which happened behind the scenes at La Scala, when a servant announced supper. Every gentleman gave his arm to a lady, and I followed with Miss Mary Bell, one of the inmates of the house, a visitor like myself. We came into the large dining-room, a beautiful room which I had not seen before, and here an elegant supper was laid for a party, which must have numbered four and twenty.

You would thank me, dear reader, if I could and would write down, for you, every word of the jolly talk ; the funny story-telling ; the grave discussion of the groups, which fell into talk and even into song as the next two hours went by. There was one very merry party around John at our end of the table. There were six or eight others around his wife at her end, with their own thread of discussion, their own bursts of laughter, and, once or twice, they commanded silence as they put up Mr. Dunning to a verse of a song. Some four or five, on each side of the table, midway, gave allegiance and attention to either of these groups, or had their own talk across the table, where no high pyramid of flowers cut off easy story-telling. And, often and often, all voices but one were lulled, as in those songs of Dunning's, or when some approved story-teller launched on some fact or fiction, which by common consent, the rest chose to hear.

What was evident, from the first minute, was, that I was the only person who was in the very least a stranger there. The others,—why one would say that they were there every week in their lives. And, before I had done with this household, I found that in fact they were.

I had chances for long, serious talk, and for much funny chaff, with this Miss Bell, whom, almost by accident, I had led out to supper. Yes, I liked her from the first, though at first I was afraid of her. I did not understand her at first. Perhaps I do not understand her now. It is so hard to understand a person who does not wholly understand herself.

She gave me some keys to the company with whom I was to make this visit. For John Fisher himself, in whose house we were, she had unmixed respect and a queer vein of familiarity side by side with strange moods of reserve. I did not in the least make it out that evening, but now I think I understand it. Of Mrs. Fisher, she would absolutely say nothing. Once and again I led the conversation that way, and, every time, I found it landed promptly on some distant shore, and before I knew it, we were talking of Madame de Sévigné, or of Cetawayo, or of Julius Cæsar. When I found out, as I did before long, that Mrs. Fisher was a fool, pure and simple, I saw why Miss Bell had been thus unwilling to discuss her with a stranger.

As to herself, Miss Bell was tall, easy in manner, a little shy in expressing herself. She was, clearly enough, used to society, and, as I found afterwards, to society in all its forms. Yet I thought then, and I know now, that if you had put her for a month in a log cabin on an Adirondack mountain, and had sent ravens to feed her, while the spring supplied her drink, she would not have found her time hang heavy. She seemed to take the society of those around her as something which she was glad to have ; yet I fancied she would not have walked two miles to seek it, if it had not happened to be there. Pretty clearly, she had not solved all her conundrums yet, and she thought some of them hard to solve. But which conundrums these were, she would not tell me, a stranger. She had not that fatal facility of confidence.

We all fairly lounged over the supper table, and nobody wanted to break the spell. It was long after midnight when Mrs. Savage rose, and said, "We shall all be as sleepy as bats to-morrow," and bade Mrs. Fisher good even-ing. This broke up the whole. The party bade good-bye in the drawing-room, and in fifteen minutes we of the household were in our bed-chambers.

Then I tried to recollect whether John Fisher had shown any musical enthusiasms in college. Had this all developed late in life? Surely he was not in the college choir, yet he would have been, had he known C sharp when he saw it. Certainly not in the glee club ! Nor had he any piano then.

But then he had not money enough, in those days, for a piano. But, leaving pianos aside, so few fellows had pianos thirty years ago. I could not recollect that John even had a jew's-harp. I did not remember that he ever whistled a tune. How strangely fellows do turn out!

Of the whole crew of us, John Fisher was the very last I should ever have thought of as President of a Jubal club and the leading virtuoso in music of a great city!

CHAPTER II.

WITH some of us breakfast is a critical business, and the prosperity of our day largely depends upon it. I was, therefore, glad enough to find that it was not shuffled out of sight, in mad haste, at John Fisher's, but recognized as the glad solemnity, not to say sacrament, which it is, loved and lingered over, and regarded indeed as the first friend of the day and not as a skirmishing enemy.

How sad the household where breakfast is simply the hasty fighting place, where the man of the household seizes a buttered roll in his hands, gulps down his cup of ruined coffee and runs for his inexorable train!

At John Fisher's, on my first morning there, I found many, many things to eat, in that American abundance which contrasts so agreeably with the "Toast, sir?" "Mutton chop, sir?" "Muffins, sir?" which constitute the stock in trade of the chef at an English inn.

More important than this, they were lavish as to time.

" I am awake now," John Fisher would say ; " and we are by ourselves, now. Heaven knows where we may be at lunch ; or who may be here at dinner, or at supper."

John Fisher had invariably been up before breakfast. He had imbibed his oxygen and his ozone on some piazza or stoop, while he read his morning paper. Perhaps he had had an early cup of coffee.

He would come into the breakfast-room among the first, throwing the newspaper away as he did, and exclaiming that there was not a word of news, and that he did not see how people could live and print such stuff.

" Now, here is a stock-broker's rumor that the Emperor of Germany has broken his leg. Why, I had a dispatch at my counting-room when I went down town yesterday, to say it was all a lie, from our own man at Vienna."

I intimated gently, that the local editor at Tamworth probably did not have " his own man " at Vienna. At which suggestion John was well pleased. The truth was, that he was so well informed a man himself, that the average "chief" of a journal would have been at disadvantage in meeting him.

" Now we will not hurry," he said, as he sat welcoming one and another arrival, after he had asked a blessing on the day. " We will not hurry. At lunch we shall have to hurry. At dinner we may have to be grand. Who knows whether there will be any supper? Here is breakfast ; this is a fixed fact. And unless the ground opens and swallows us up, we are well-nigh sure.

" What do you say? Do you begin with fruit? Or there is oatmeal on the side-table. Miss Bell will give you ome-

lette ; or, I will give you a piece of steak ; or, there is fish.
That white fish is fresh. Jonas brought it in, while I put
on my necktie."

And then he began talking. On this particular morning,
he was in excellent spirits. He was never in bad spirits,
indeed. But sometimes he talked more gayly than at others,
and this was one of these times.

"What I mean, Cordelia, is this," said he. He had
been talking with her on the piazza, before breakfast. "It
is a great waste of capital, by which you story-tellers introduce a new hero, a new heroine ; or, a new second hero, or
new second heroine ; a new villain's tool and a new villain's
fool, with every story you tell. I hardly know their names,
I am so stupid, before you wind up the book.

"Then I have to buy a new book, and to learn another
set of names.

"Now if my business were story writing,—and I sometimes wish it were,—I would do as the Chinese do with
their plays. I would let the story run on and on, just as
life does. People could begin to read where they like, and
leave off where they like, as they do at that Normal School
in Ohio which you told about. They need not buy the
early numbers, and they need not hold on till my death.

"Indeed, when I died I would leave the good-will of my
story, as David Crockett did his almanac."

"How was that?" said Mrs. Grattan, laughing.

"Why, there was a comic almanac published, called
'Crockett's Almanac,' full of hunting stories, alligator fights,
and so on,—very popular among boys like me, and Tom
there. One unfortunate day, Davy Crockett was killed at
Alamo, if you know what that was?"

Mrs. Grattan shook her head for "no," like a guilty thing.

"No matter. He was killed. But the almanac appeared all the same. And it bore the statement that he had 'completed the preparations, calculations and all, for five years in advance, before he ever went to Texas.'

"Now that is the way to start a novel."

I said some German said that the Iliad has no introduction and no conclusion, that it is just like a Greek frieze. The head of a horse sticks in at the left, and the tail of a horse sticks out at the right, and it is supposed that you know that the head has a tail and the tail has a head.

"Just so," said John. "A sensible German. Find his address and I will send him our new illustrated catalogue from the shop. I do not doubt he will give us an order."

Mary Bell said that Trollope did work in this way, so far as his inferior people go. The background of his story is always familiar ground.

"Exactly," said John Fisher, "and that is why we everyday working people liked Trollope so much. And when I found from his book that he reeled off novels, as I do machinery, twelve pages every day he lived; glad or sorry, sick or well, at sea or at home; one steady, twelve-page grind, why I could have kissed him, and I would, if he would appear to me a vision. He wrote novels as the British government built gunboats."

"How was that?" asked Cordelia Grattan.

"You are so good-natured. You have heard me tell twenty times. Thank you for being so civil. They used to build a long trough of gunboat out into the sea. Then, when an order came for a new gunboat, why, they cut off eighty-six feet and fastened on a ready-made bow and a ready-made stern, and sent her to sea; had another ready-made bow and stern for the next, and so on. They could deliver a great many in a week."

"I wish you would write a novel," said Mrs. Grattan. "You would not be near so hard on us who do."

"Take care, or I will. The very first day the mail fails, so that I have no letters; bridge broken at Taladega; snow drift at Girard, I will call Miss Typewriter,—her real name is Jones,—and I will begin :

"'James could not hold in his anger at this announcement.' And I tell you the public will start, when they find such a prompt beginning as that, and when the chapter ends with 'Hector!' she cried, as she found the treacherous sods gave way, and she was falling through space——'

"Will they not be uneasy, then, till the next chapter arrives, in the next number of The Century?

"But that is what life is. Heavens! am I not now going down town to have a cable from 'London tell me that Mr. Gladstone has been struck in the head by a paving-stone? And then the dispatch will stop. And if he dies, all values will decline, and I shall stop the works and we shall all retire to that log-cabin in Purchasville, which is the property of Cordelia's uncle, and shall live there on ground nuts.

"And if he lives, all values will boom, and I shall present to each of you a diamond necklace for a birthday present.

"You are all, always, sitting on the edge of such a volcano; and yet you think William Black's guidebook stories interesting, and talk to me of the plot of the Duchess's farrago. Lucky for you that I do not write novels."

"Indeed, indeed!" said Mrs. Grattan. "I shall pray for a snow-drift at Girard. Once you try with your Miss Jones, you will wish you had forty of your old letters to answer. Stay at home to-day, and help my hero out of his scrapes. I will go to the office, and your Miss Jones and I will see to the mail."

No, John Fisher would not do that. But he said he would take us all to the office, and then if I liked I might take the ladies to drive. He would leave the carriage and horses with us. We might call for him at one o'clock and he would come home to lunch. And to this we gladly agreed.

By the ladies were meant Mrs. Fisher and Miss Mary Bell. We were to start in half an hour. We left the breakfast-table for family prayers. Fisher read a few verses from the Bible; we all offered the Lord's Prayer, and with Mrs. Grattan at the piano, sang two verses of a hymn. Every one disappeared with the understanding that we were to meet for our drive in half an hour.

CHAPTER III.

IN half an hour Fisher and I stood on the steps, and Miss Bell joined us. But word came down from Mrs. Fisher that she was too busy, and would not come. Neither of the others seemed surprised.

"Go ask Mrs. Grattan if she would like to ride," said

Fisher to the maid. " Say there is an empty seat, if she likes it."

To my surprise, Mrs. Grattan appeared immediately, ready for the drive, as if she had been expected. I found afterwards, that whenever Mrs. Fisher said she would go, she did not; and whenever she declined, she afterwards changed her mind, like the boys in the parable. It made no inconvenience, for every one in the house calculated absolutely on this habit of hers.

Like most men who have lived much in action in the open air, Fisher liked to drive his own horses, rather than to have a coachman drive them. A great carriage builder once told me, that he had to devise special carriages for the need of men of wealth who want to be their own coachmen. I sympathize with the men of wealth.

Fisher discovered a short cut which took us off the crowded street at once, and in a minute he was in the gayest talk as he drove to his works, perhaps a mile out of town. Then he called a lad to stand by the horses, and asked me to come in for a moment to see his workshop.

" You need not leave the carriage," he said to the ladies. " This is an old story to you, and I will not keep him two minutes."

He wanted to show me a particular contrivance for the transfer of power, of which we had been talking, and, with just a nod to the people we met, he led the way to the long, low room where we could see this. We were talking all the way about people and things.

I saw the bit of machinery; I understood the difficulties and the success enough to ask the right questions about it. I heard part of what he said, and three-quarters of it I lost,

in the whirr of wheels, the stamping of hammers, and the
trill of saws. When we came out on the stairway, he said :

" Her fortune was enormous then, and it is larger now.
And really, all she wants to know is how to spend the
income of it, for the good of man and the love of God. You
see she is as simple in her taste and dress as if she were my
typewriter."

It would have been better, perhaps, had I asked whom
he was talking about. But I did not like to, and I had
not a moment to think. Probably it was one of the ladies
in the carriage. For I had spoken of Miss Mary Bell
before the clatter had begun.

I was no fool, and I should find out before our drive was
over.

" I leave you with the ladies," he said. " There are
one hundred and six different drives from this place, each
more lovely than the other."

" What they do not know about them is not worth
knowing. So, bon voyage ! "

" Be prompt at one, Mrs. Grattan, or I will dictate two
novels."

And so we started.

CHAPTER IV.

I MUST not describe the drive. If I do we shall never
be done.

I told the ladies that they meant to pile all their treasures
together. Mary Bell was an enthusiast in the open air.
Her complete knowledge of the outer world and sympathy

with everything that has life made a curious contrast with a certain quietness of manner as we sat talking at home.

Mrs. Grattan, as perhaps became a novel-writer, was an enthusiast and a dreamer in her way. But she did not pretend to know any difference but that of color between the purple of ripened grasses as the sun struck them, and the brown of sedge in a swamp, such as could hardly be found elsewhere on that side of the Mississippi.

" No, Mary," she would say, " it is quite enough that one of us knows these things. You shall expound and explain to me and when I forget, for I shall forget, you shall expound again ; and you are so good, Mary, that you will not mind if I make you tell me twenty times."

Under the direction of these two fanatics I drove the bays, that morning, up hill and down dale, across the table-land, through swamps, by the side of brooks, to this " shed line " and that, for twenty different points of observation. We passed by hill-sides where the purple grasses grew, we passed across meadows where late asters grew, we got glimpses of the blue of the far-away hills, we caught the reflection of red maples in a dozen different lakes, and came round by the usual cemetery, established on the site of an old Indian battle-ground. Of all this I must tell no detail, but rather what I learned, such as it was, of the life and fortunes of my college friend, John Fisher.

" You are here to speak to the Temperance people, are you not?" said Mrs. Grattan to me as we came to a long causeway, where for a minute, even Mary Bell had no botanizing to rave about, nor distant cumulus to wonder at.

" Yes," I said, " I had agreed to speak at a great meeting which was to be held before the election, and when

Fisher heard of this he wrote to me that I was to come direct from Omaha and make this visit, which had been talked of now for nearly thirty years."

" Is he especially interested in this temperance matter?" I asked. " Why, of course he is," said Mrs. Grattan, looking at me with her great wondering eyes, as she might have looked had I asked if John Fisher knew the names of his own children. " Live in Tamworth long enough, and you will not have to ask such questions; or go down every morning as he did just now, to tell thirteen hundred men what they are to do before dinner, and you will see why he is interested."

" Yes," I said, a little impatiently; " but is he interested in it as he is interested in music, or as you are interested in novel-writing?"

" John Fisher interested in music?" asked Mrs. Grattan, lifting her eye-brows. And Mary Bell turned round on me as if I had confounded him with some other man.

" Why surely," I said, " last night——"

" Oh, yes! last night," said Mrs. Grattan, and then both the ladies laughed. " Wait till you see to-night, and wait till you see to-morrow night.

" John Fisher is interested in music just as he is interested in books and athletics, and pretty houses with clematis over the window, and reading clubs, and pictures, and ice-chests in the milk shops, and cheap cottons and good cutlery, and in anything else that helps toward the ' good time coming,' or, as he would say, ' to make the Kingdom of God come.' But how he would laugh if he knew you thought him an authority on music because we happened to go to the Jubal together."

"Well," said Mary Bell, "I wish I had his knack, or you may call it his gift. I wish I knew how to help people without ruining them in the helping. Seriously, we might do a worse thing than to start him upon writing his novel."

"Novel!" cried Cordelia Grattan. "The man's whole life is one romance. But it is quite too varied to be written down. It defies all the unities at once. Indeed, it needs a steady hand like his to keep those forty-seven prancing steeds of the Sun in any sort of order."

"Steeds of the Sun?" asked I. "And is there no twilight, no shadow, no darkness in his life?"

They hesitated for a moment, both. But after a moment, Mrs. Grattan said gravely, "I should think there was;" and at the same instant Mary Bell said, almost in a, whisper, "You will see." We were all embarrassed, and I, to relieve the stiffness and to change the subject safely, asked Miss Bell if she were any relation to the Mary Bell of the Rollo Books. But at that moment, passing out through a chestnut grove we came in sight of the chimneys of the factory, and Miss Bell pointed at them.

"I must tell you that another time," said she. "Here we are."

CHAPTER V.

"AND how have your romances sped?" This was John Fisher's question, as soon as he had gathered the reins in his hands. "Did a horde of red-skins in their war-paint rise shouting from a morass to scalp you? And did Tom here empty two revolvers among their number,

not missing once in his unerring aim ; and then touching
up his gallant bays, did he rescue all from impending danger, and receive in reward the guerdon of Miss Mary's
hand, or Mrs. Grattan's?

"Not that I know what a guerdon is," he added, in
mock meditative tone.

The ladies laughed, and we owned that we had only
added descriptive passages, heavy padding, to our stories ;
but Mrs. Grattan asked eagerly what was the progress of
his.

John Fisher took on a more serious air, and he said that
if we did not object to extending our drive to the Look-out
Station and back, that would give him fifteen minutes, and
so he told the story.

Mrs. Flaherty had come in. "You know her, Cordelia.
Husband that drunken brute. This time he had been off
longer than usual,—thank God for that! But last night,
late, came a letter from somebody in Chicago. How those
people get their letters, if indeed they ever do get the right
ones, I never knew.

"Anyhow, here was the letter, black and white ; very
bad spelling, announcing that Tim Flaherty, who is supposed to be her Tim, got into a drunken fight last month,
stabbed a policeman who died, and that Tim is now in the
state prison for fourteen years. For once, they seem to
have given short shrift in Chicago."

"That is the best news I have heard in a month," said
Mary Bell, quietly.

"I made the same observation to his wife," said John.
"But I am sorry to say it made her cry. Now, a more
gentle spirit, say Cordelia here, would have encouraged

her, would have said that there are forty-seven Tim Flahertys in the directory, and maybe it was not he.

" I boldly said I was sure it was he, and that I was very glad, and so I made her cry.

" But I told her that this was as good as a divorce,—these people call them ' disvoces,'—and better. I told her that now she was in no more danger of paying his whisky bills. I asked her whether my bookkeeper had anything to her credit. You see, Tom, this is the woman who washes the towels, and makes things tidy in the counting-rooms, and her fortunes are the common interest of Miss Bell and me.

" They occupy me much more than the Emperor of Russia's order does," he added, laughing.

Then, in answer to Mrs. Grattan's eager and detailed questions, it proved that the bookkeeper had saved four or five weeks of her earnings from the grasp of different bar-room princes, to whom Flaherty had given orders for her money. There were twenty odd dollars to her credit.

"Then we sent to the annealing room for Dan. Dan came, and he made a fine appearance, Mrs. Grattan. He does credit to your artistic eye, Mary. I recognized your taste in the very color of his overalls. Dan reported that his foreman had,—oh! I think forty dollars to his credit. Between them they had held this in face of orders unnumbered signed by Tim. To tell the truth, I am afraid they had lied awfully, in a good cause. But the money had not been passed over.

" On which, I bade Dan go and make himself decent, and told the foreman he must get along without him this morning. Then Dan went in the glory of a clean face and of his Sunday hat to find up Kilmansegg. Kilmansegg was on the top of a load of lumber. But Dan hailed him, tendered his hundred dollars, and Kilmansegg said it was right, and that he should have the deed before night, and he will."

Of this condensed narrative I asked the explanation. It proved that Kilmansegg was treasurer of a Building Association. That Dan and his mother had coveted a certain five-room house which belonged to this Association. But they had not dared to buy while Tim could pounce on their wages at any moment.

Now that Tim was "jugged," in the elegant phrase of his first-born, the mother and son were able to go into their first real estate speculation.

"You said a hundred dollars," said Mary Bell, breaking her part of the silence. "But you only accounted for sixty odd."

John Fisher blushed, as if he had been detected in a crime. "Oh, the foreman and I made that all right. I told them they must work and they will. 'Real Estate' means a great deal, Tom. Your only way to help people is to show them how to help themselves, and the real,— 'royal' I suppose the word means, step to helping themselves, is over real estate. None of your sham estates, as Mary Stevenson said of the roast pork. What is your story about Antæus, Miss Bell?"

"I did not know it was my story."

"Well, the explanation of it is, that whenever he was in the stock-market and the bears pulled him down, Antæus fell back on his real estate investments. He put his foot on the earth, and as I heard the parson say one day: 'He drank in new strength from his mother.'

" Dan Flaherty will never drink. Sixty dollars a year will he save which would else go in whisky. The sons of these drunken dogs almost invariably hate IT." John Fisher always spoke of whisky as " It," with a certain jerk, which I represent by a large I. "They hate IT. It is their children, the boys and girls too, who sometimes have the curse in their blood, poor things.

" But now, Dan and his mother have fairly started on the ascent of the Great Temple, or Tower, or Castle of Human Life. It is built on Real Estate. And when success is ended for all four of us, and we are poor beggars, all of us seeking a day's crust, we will hand in hand knock at the door of the Flaherty palace, and they shall take us in."

And so he swept up to the door of his own palace, and gave the reins to the waiting groom.

CHAPTER VI.

THE party at lunch was as large as that had been at supper the night before. But I did not recognize one face of those who met then, except the children of the house and the ladies. There was a certain informality about the gathering as becomes a party at lunch : a great deal of merriment, as was natural where most of the guests were young, and talk irrepressible.

No! If I had expected musical amateurs again, and I

did not after the ladies' laughter in the morning, I should
have been disappointed. It very soon appeared that the
party was made up mostly from the Directors and other
officers of the Base Ball Nine of Tamworth, who had come
with their wives, and, in some cases, with their daughters,
and with whom were other gentlemen interested in the
Athletics of the town. The Medical Director of the Gym-
nasium was there; the President of the Cricket Club was
there: a white-cravated, single-breasted young man, who
proved to be the minister of St. George's church. They
were prayer-book people, and, being Americans, said "Minister" and did not say "Rector." The head of the High School
was there; the President of the Rowing Club, and in short
we were a company of very muscular Christians, with their
pretty wives and daughters.

No! the talk was not very much of the shop. We were
going in the afternoon to see a practice game, as it was
called, of the Tamworth Club, who were to exhibit themselves in full rig, to their admiring friends, after a tour
they had made through the principal towns in the State, in
which they had easily maintained their championship as
the best club in the State, a championship which they had
now held for several years.

I observed that we all spoke as if it were a matter of
course that our club should hold the championship. Nor
was this the last time that I observed, that, whatever the
subject of conversation, the Tamworth people all understood, that they stood, as it were, of course, in a well-
defined position of leadership. Had the Chief Justice died
in the night, I am quite clear that the men of Tamworth,
as they met at the post-office the next day, would have

determined promptly which of the Tamworth lawyers could
be best spared to go to Washington and to take his place.
I remembered that last night, when I had said that something was better played than I had ever heard it, the large-
eyed woman to whom I spoke, had intimated that this was
quite a matter of course. But I had not then understood,
as I came to do, before the week was over, that this was
not her notion only, but that it was the happy habit of all
the town.

So, all through lunch, it was "conceded" that the jour-
ney of the club had been an unnecessary courtesy, due in a
sort to the other cities and towns of the State. The "boys"
had of course done well, and now the afternoon was to be
made a fête day in their honor.

As I say, the talk was not very largely on base ball.
But it was very Aryan. Or, not to speak philologically, it
was all quick with ozone, oxygen and the open air. You
were ashamed of yourself, if you were not in the habit of
walking fifteen miles a day. It was taken for granted that
you knew the "record" for bicycles and tricycles, and that
for amateurs as distinguished from professionals. You did
not speak of a boat, but, in more precise phrase, of a birch,
or a canoe, a shell, or a four-oar, or a catamaran, or a cat,
or some one other of forty different builds. It was taken for
granted that life was very well worth living, and you would
have said that not one of these very brown and very handsome young people had ever had an ache or a pain.

I was a little annoyed to find that Miss Bell was not at
the table. "One of her Bible-class called on her at just the
wrong time," said Cordelia Grattan. I had hoped that I
might sit by her at table, and that she should be guide,

philosopher and friend, to explain to me the different guests, and interpret to me the local jokes, to which, inferior, I could not mount alone.

Instead of this, I was introduced to a stranger, with whom to begin all over again, as I had begun with Mary Bell, the night before. To borrow the simple phrase of the Georgia colonel, I was " put out to a strange gal."

But poor Mary Bell was less pleasantly engaged than we were. The Mrs. Waters who had called on her was evidently ill at ease from the first. It took her some time before she could come to her story.

" I am so sorry I interrupt you. I see Mrs. Fisher has company. Oh, no! I would not think of staying. I am not dressed, you know! Indeed, indeed, Miss Bell! I would not have waited for you, if—well, you will see, I had to wait, if it was any good coming at all."

" The dumb man's borders still increase."

This is a favorite quotation of Mary Bell, and to a considerable extent, it accounts for what people think a certain reserve in her manner. But as the Mrs. Waters stammered and stopped, and blushed, and turned pale, Mary Bell began to think that even this great principle of life was going to fail her.

" You are sure no one hears us? Did any one mention my name?" These ejaculations followed from the visitor, as for the second time she tried the door, and made sure that it was fast.

Then with a bold dash she said, " Do you know anything about Mrs. Fisher's necklace, her opal necklace? Has she said anything about it to you?"

Then Mary Bell remembered what she had hardly had any

occasion to know, that the husband of Mrs. Waters was the chief man in the large shop of Niederkranz & Smith, the chief jewelry firm of Tamworth. Mr. Niederkranz was old and lame, and never appeared. Mr. Smith was in the counting-room or somewhere, and seldom appeared. Mr. Waters was perhaps the " Co."—anyhow he was the man you always saw.

And at last, with much difficulty, many surprises, endless parentheses and other obstructions, Mrs. Waters told Miss Bell that nearly twelve months before, Mrs. Fisher had brought to the firm this necklace, which she did not want repaired; she did not want to sell; she wanted to pledge for money. She wanted a large sum of money for private use; some relatives she wanted to befriend, and it was to be, for the time, a secret from her husband. She did not like to have to ask him for the money, she said. But there was this necklace, which had cost five thousand dollars at Tiffany's. She brought Tiffany's bill as her evidence. Would they lend her a thousand dollars for two or three months, and take the necklace as security? Mr. Waters had received this precious confidence. Mr. Waters had been a good deal disgusted, not to say mortified. But he had asked Mr. Smith, who was rather a cynic, and woman-hater. He had laughed, and had said it was a pity not to accommodate so good a customer. Ten bank bills, of one hundred dollars each, had been given to Mrs. Fisher, and she had the next day sent down the necklace.

The queer part of the story was that nobody had looked at it. The box was marked with Tiffany's name. Mr. Waters was busy and thought Mr. Smith had looked at it. Mr. Smith was cross and thought Mr. Waters had looked at it. A boy had been bidden to carry it to the safe and had locked it up. At the end of three months, or thereabouts, Mrs. Fisher had been reminded of the loan, and she had said, " in a few days." At the end of three months more, she had said "in a few days" again; and so in three months more. There had come a row. Old Mr. Niederkranz had been jumbled down to the store in his carriage to look at the accounts. He had seen the entry of one thousand dollars lent to Mrs. Fisher, in a little private cash-book. He had asked a question, pretty cross. The pledged jewel had been sent for. The box had been opened, and lo! a trinket of brass and copper and glass, not even up to Attleborough standards, such as the grand Tiffany never dreamed of, even in a nightmare!

Of course every one was amazed. Every one felt abused. Every one threw the blame on every one else. Mr. Niederkranz was opposed in politics to Mr. Fisher. He swore he would expose him. Mr. Smith was cross; he always was cross. This time he had been good-natured, and see what had come of it! Mr. Waters was the only person who was in the least cool. He did not know what was to be done. Therefore he consulted his wife, having begged a truce, or intermission of hostilities till afternoon. Mrs. Waters did not know what should be done, but had ordered her carriage and had come to tell Mary Bell, and leave the responsibility with her.

For Mary Bell, as I had many occasions afterwards to learn, is one of those persons on whom everybody throws the responsibility. It would be one thing if this were only the responsibility of judging what other people should do, as for instance the Pope does. But in Mary Bell's case, and in other like cases, I have observed that certain people not only have to decide as to duty, but have to bell the cat. " I told Mary Bell," people say, and then they fancy that they have nothing more to do in the premises. She will take the whole affair off their hands, not that she wants to, poor woman. " But then, you will do it so much better than I, Miss Bell." As probably she will.

Such was Mary Bell's occupation while the rest of us were at lunch before the athletic exhibition, or reception of our nine. She was hearing, weighing, and learning to understand Mrs. Waters's incredible story.

CHAPTER VII.

NO! I will not be tempted by any artistic considerations to switch off from the proper track of this story, too much crowded at the best, to tell the fortunes of that afternoon's game of base ball. How Fremantle covered himself with glory by very prettily stealing second, or how Dawes disgusted every one by curious lack of judgment in throwing to bases, but subsequently made up a little by striking out seven men consecutively. All this has its place in literature, as Dr. Everett and a certain unknown author in the No Name series have shown. There will yet be published a novel in which every one's destiny will turn on the question whether, as the Hector of the story springs from the ground, stretching his arm above him, his fingers close tightly on the ball, or whether the ball strikes the third phalangette, breaks it backward and disables him for life. On this shall hinge the fortunes of the blonde heroine and the brunette heroine; of the cynical hero and the good-natured hero; of the man of millions and the beggar in the gutter. But this story is not that novel, and I sadly pass by the fascinating episode.

The reader will lay down the book, and recall the last game he say played on the Diamond Field; will imagine that the party from Mr. Fisher's is sitting, watching the players, in three or four open carriages; will observe that John Fisher is not there, but that Mrs. Fisher is; rather noisy, rather simple in her observations, and always foolish, and then the reader will return from the ball-ground to the house.

And here was to be a party in-doors and out-doors, for all the players, for all the substitutes, for the amateur clubs and all their friends. The party was to be in-doors if it rained; out-doors if it were not too cold. And, as it proved, it was one of the last straggling days of Indian summer, and on the exquisite lawn were scattered groups of pretty girls who had not yet lost the brown of their summer campaign, and of eager boys who were browner than the dames they admired. A band of music was on the west terrace, and just before the sun went down, in answer to a suggestion of Cordelia Grattan's, the dignity of the great leader of the music so far unbent that he consented to play a waltz; nay, many waltzes. The hint was readily taken, and boys and girls, young men and maidens; nay, gentlemen of nine-and-fifty and women of an uncertain age, were flying round and round on that almost matchless lawn, "accoutred as they were," and enjoying the dance all the more because they danced in boots and hats and bonnets.

For myself, I had determined, as I dressed for the party, that I would devote myself to our hostess, and find out, if I could, why thus far I knew so little of her. I saw her talking with a young man, who seemed ill at ease, and I drew up to them, thinking that he might wish to be relieved, and she be equally grateful if I relieved him.

I was at least half right. As for the rest, I do not know.

"I think not," he said, as I drew near. Either he was of a very florid complexion or he was blushing vehemently.

"Oh! yes it is,—I know it is," cried Mrs. Fisher, and she giggled vehemently. "I tell all the young men so."

"What do you tell them?" asked I. I never knew any one who did not class himself among the young men. Certainly I am one of them. Dr. Jackson says the prime of life lasts till we are sixty-five.

"I tell Mr. Rose he should have his eye-glass set with diamonds. They have such pretty ones at Bookwalter's."

"And I tell Mrs. Fisher," said young Rose, "that she must have our salaries raised at the Board of Works." And then, quite as much relieved as I had fancied he would be, he touched his hat, and walked away. But it was pretty clear to me that he had been a little wounded by his hostess.

I asked where her husband was. "He affects to be at leisure all the afternoon," said I. "Can he not come and help in the dancing?"

"Don't ask me about Mr. Fisher. He goes his way, and I go mine. I tell him if he will not bother me about his old machinery, and his letters from Europe, and the price of iron, I will not bother him when I give a party."

Of which ready retort, the specially interesting feature was that it was wholly untrue. Not only had Mrs. Fisher never made any such remark, which had in fact flashed on her at the moment, but every arrangement for this party had been made by John Fisher himself. The band had been ordered; the collation had been provided; the invitations had been written and sent, all as one little detail in the business of this particular day. And, because he was a great man of business, the very smallest of them and the largest had all been attended to ten days before.

"He likes young people, does he not?" This was my next attempt.

"Oh, yes! I suppose he does. I am sure he is always filling up the house with them. It is a party to-day, and a reception to-morrow, and an afternoon tea next day. I say to them that I might just as well be keeping a hotel. Better, indeed, for there's Jane Mulhouse,—she does keep a hotel, or her husband does. And she lives in just the sweetest, dearest little house, on a side street in Chicago, with her books and her birds and her music, and you would not know there was a hotel within a thousand miles of her. That's the way I wish I could live." And she rolled her eyes over her fan at me, with a sentimental look which gave me courage. For I saw that even I was worth flirting with. I persevered.

"I was sorry you could not go on our drive with us to-day. Mrs. Grattan said you were not well."

"Oh, yes! I had one of my headaches. I am not fit to be here now. But it is one of the things,—well, I suppose you orators would say,—it is one of the things which one owes to society. That means, Mr. Mellen," she said in an affected sadness, "that means that my husband chooses to give a great party, and tells his people to invite Tom, Dick, and Harry, whom I never saw nor heard of, and then wants me to come and be gracious to them all, and make it pass off well. Well, I do as I am bidden. That is poor woman's place, I suppose. What is a headache to compare with the good of society?" And she sighed profoundly.

I saw that I had made a mistake, and I stumbled out of it as well as I could. " You spoke of your friend's quiet life with her books. I suppose I may credit you for those charming editions I saw in the breakfast-room."

I took her off her guard here. For the moment she hesitated, doubting whether she would say she had selected them or not. But the instinct for contradiction prevailed, as it almost always does with silly women, badly bred or not bred at all. They seem to think that there is wit, or at least brilliancy, in opposing every proposition brought forward.

"Books? Oh! breakfast-room? Oh, yes! I know what you mean. Oh, no! Don't charge me with filling the whole house up with books. I may do very silly things. I believe people think I do. But the book folly was never one of mine. I tell them that I have my Bible, and my cook-books, and that if they want to talk about French novels, or German philosophers, they must go to some one else. Books, indeed! I pity the maids who have to dust them, and for all me they might be carved out of oak, as some books were which I saw somewhere."

" That does very well for you to say," I said, persevering, as one sometimes does, because the exigencies of social life seem to require it. " For all that, I should like to have a peep at the table in your own sitting-room and see who your favorite authors are."

"No, you would not, Mr. Mellen. You would find my favorite authors are people you turned up your nose at. I am not one of the people who run with the crowd. My husband made me go to the theatre to see the Lady of Lyons. 'Why should I see the Lady of Lyons?' I said. Then the next night they had something of Shakspere's. I would not go; just to show my independence I would not go. I hate Shakspere, and I said I did. Then the man acted something else, Claude Melnotte, was it not? and I went to that just because the others would not. No, you would not want to see my favorite authors."

I said I had been turning over the music in the music racks, and I saw that she had some of my special favorites there.

"Music! I fond of music? Did you really think because my poor husband chose to fill the house with those people, squalling and howling last night, that I cared for music? In the first place, I cannot sing a note. And, in the second place, I never had any patience to practice when I was a girl. And in the third place I have no ear. Oh, dear! Mr. Mellen, the money that is spent in this city on singers and players, operas and concerts, terrifies me. If I had my way, there should not be a jews-harp in the town."

I was beginning to wonder what was the charm of that Chicago lady's house, seeing books and music, on which I had ventured first, were so worthless. I believe I should have asked if Mr. Fisher were fond of birds, but another lady drew near, paid her respects, and the two fell into talk together, in which I was an unwilling third. But I had not, or thought I had not, a chance to leave.

"So glad to see you, Mrs. Vanderweyer."

"So glad to see you, dear Mrs. Fisher. What a perfect day you have, and what a lovely party."

"It is pretty to see the young people, is it not? I was saying to Mr. Mellen,—let me introduce Mr. Mellen,—that there is nothing I so delight in as seeing young people happy. I hope dear Clara is here."

No; Clara was out of town. She had gone over to the college at New Padua, and there was an exhibition that day, and Clara had stayed to hear Dr. Farrar read Browning.

"Dr. Farrar read Browning!" cried Mrs. Fisher. "Do you tell me that to-day is the day for Browning? Why, I sent over for the tickets a week ago, and they lie on my table now. I so dote on Browning. I was saying to Mr. Mellen that if I could not call Browning my own poet, and Christina Rossetti, too, you know, I did not think life would be worth living."

Mrs. Vanderweyer had undoubtedly heard enough of such protestations before. She broke in a little unceremoniously to ask where Mr. Fisher was.

"Don't ask me about John Fisher. I am the last person in Tamworth to ask about him. I tell them that everybody else is privileged to know about him, except poor I. No! this is just the way. He comes to me and says, 'It is time for a party to the people of the town.' And I say I think it will be a pretty time for a lawn party. Then I order the music, and send out my notes, and put on my best gown, and come and have the party, and John Fisher has forgotten all about it. He is down at the foundry with a new steam gauge, or he is in the Club talking politics, and I have the party to entertain. I say to them that at the end of the year he does not know his neighbors by sight, he is so unsociable."

And so on, and so on.

And in truth, all this afternoon John Fisher was sadly and wearily rushing from one office to another and one house to another, to hear more and more details of her utter folly and absurdity, in her fraud with the necklace, and was trying to save her from the public disgrace which at twelve o'clock that day had seemed inevitable.

For Mary Bell, unwillingly enough, had gone to him to tell him the whole story. It was certainly the best thing which she could do.

CHAPTER VIII.

OF all this misery about the necklace, I knew nothing all that afternoon, nor, indeed, for some days after.

The day was only too short for the dancers. But the evening chill would come on, and unwillingly enough they retreated to the house. There a few enthusiastic couples still kept up their waltzing, with a band not at all unwilling. To my great pleasure Mary Bell appeared. I felt more at ease with her than I did with any one but our host. I saw this afternoon that she was a little ill at ease. But when I asked after him, she simply said that his time was never his own, and that she supposed some one had called him away.

Just as the last dancers disappeared he came in. If he were annoyed or careworn, I did not then notice it, nor learn that he was tired. The very moment when the last guest vanished, "tea" was announced. It proved to be that composite meal which old housekeepers call a "high tea," where, on one hospitable board, appear provisions which would answer for breakfast, lunch, dinner, tea or supper, or for all of these piled together. The children were here and their father let them have their way; he drew them out, indeed. Perhaps he did not want to show that he himself had something other than hospitality to think of. At all events he did not show it then.

We really lounged at table, listening to the boys' accounts of Fremantle's prowess, and to criticisms of Dawes's wretched failure, till a servant announced that two gentlemen were waiting for Mr. Fisher in the library. He turned to me and asked if I would join them. "They are both intelligent men," he said, "and there will be a dozen others like them. Come if you want to talk politics. If you do not, Mrs. Fisher and Mrs. Grattan will give you some music. To tell you the truth, this is our last chance for a final discussion before our great battle of Tuesday. You have not heard, perhaps, that Tuesday week is the critical day of all history,—that Waterloo and Pharsalia only led up to it."

I said I had heard that they had their city election on that Tuesday, in fact I supposed my Temperance speech had something to do with it, and that I should be very glad to be admitted behind the scenes.

"As for that," said John Fisher as we left the room, "there is very little scenery; and very little costume, but what we wear in the shops. The English of it is, as in all large towns of which I know anything, that the liquor dealers, large and small, are of course a unit in all politics. Their business compels them to be a unit. It is just as slavery made the fifty thousand slaveholders into one great corporation, and they needed no charter to incorporate them. Of course, also, this liquor-dealing unit controls a great many votes of men who drink daily. Every chalk-score gives a lien on some one voter, and any candidate, who will wipe out that score, may have that man's vote, without many questions. Of course this combination, this unit, votes together. It votes for the same President, for the same Governor, for the same Sheriff, for the same Aldermen. There is not a large town in America where this Unit does not exist. It makes in each town a political club, of people who never saw or heard of each other. This club votes, as it has a right to, as one.

"What is there on the other side?" he went on, after he had presented me to Lauderdale and Jackson, who were waiting for us in the library. "On the other side are all sorts of opinions. There are the politicians, who are interested in National parties. They detest local politics, because they introduce so much confusion in calculations. Then there are the Temperance people. They are apt to be quarrelling with each other's panaceas. There are a handful of people, one in fifty, who care about the schools. There are a few lawyers with theories about government, and a few persons with other theories. There are some ambitious young men who wish the city were better governed; who hate rings, and will do anything, so they are only sure nobody else wants them to do it. All this breaks up the opposition to the Unit. It breaks it up so badly in some places, that the decent people, who would be glad to see a decent government, lose all heart.

They tell me that in Boston, where I think your father came from, they cannot get fifty voters in a hundred to the polls at their city elections. They tell me that the Unit governs them, while it has not a quarter part of the voters."

"But we do not do things in that way here," said Mr. Lauderdale, a fat, bustling, jolly man, who stood, with his back to the fire, rubbing his hands with glee.

"Not much," said Mr. Jackson, a tall, thin, pale man, more taciturn, to whom he appealed.

John Fisher introduced me to these two gentlemen, and I found they knew my name. Lauderdale began at once to give me points which he wished I would make in the address I had come to deliver; and Jackson, in his short-metre way, made his suggestions and confirmed his friend's. One and another gentleman came in, and to each I was presented. Some of them fell into our group, which was discussing Temperance specially, the others fell into groups of their own, all standing, until the entry of two gentlemen made our number fourteen complete, and then without even a word from our host every man looked for a chair, turned it round and seated himself, so that we all sat in a rude horseshoe order, with John Fisher in the middle, at his writing table.

"I am glad to see you all," he said, very quietly. "I hope all the news is as good as Weemyss brings us." And he looked inquiringly at the left end of the horseshoe, and nodded to the gentleman who sat there, who was, as it happened, one of the last comers.

"I am very sorry to say our news is very bad," replied he ; "it is as bad as it can be. In fact Ward 7 has gone all to pieces, and 'all the Kings oxen' cannot set it up again. If the rest of you have as bad news as I, we may as well all go a-fishing to-morrow morning."

There was something amusing in the lugubrious tone of this Mr. Harkness. But he was evidently badly in earnest. It was clear enough that he would not have made any such confession outside these sacred walls. What he was telling, also, was news which the public would not know till the next morning ; might not know for many days. But there was no doubt it was true. It amounted to this, that in the Seventh Ward, which was the very palladium of the vote of the good sense and integrity of Tamworth, on which the leaders in this coterie always relied for a square thousand majority over "It," with which to to start all their calculations, in this redoubtable Seventh Ward, certain old-time jealousies had become uncontrollable. The Blues and the Greens, in the house of our friends, were in raging quarrel with each other. Swinton had declared that he would be alderman this year, if every other district in Tamworth chose the Devil and his saints to be aldermen. Swinton would not be "sat upon" and despised any longer. He had led the ward, in good times and bad times, and he would not be snubbed as he had been at the caucus which chose delegates to the State convention. Ever since that time had this fire been smouldering in Michael Swinton's mind. And now it burst out, and there was not a man in all the shops but thought Swinton had the right of it, and deserved justice.

But, as everybody who sat around John Fisher's table

knew, that is, every one excepting me, Michael Swinton could no more be chosen the alderman of Ward 7, than Benedict Arnold could. Harkness was dramatic and very amusing, as he described the horror of the people on the Hill at any such suggestion. The people on the Hill were going to the caucus this very night, in forces such as the Hill had never sent to any caucus since caucuses were heard of. To tell the truth, the people on the Hill generally let caucuses alone. They generally voted for the ticket which was suggested,—well, in the room we were sitting in, or which was approved there. But there came occasions when the people on the Hill forgot their cosmogonies and their correlations, turned a cruel back on their own whist parties, left the discussion of Protoplasm and of Evolution ; the last novel was on the shelf, and the last *Fortnightly* was uncut, while Mr. Molineux bade Dennis drive him down to the ward meeting, that he might take part in the government of the country. This was one of these gilded occasions. There would be quiet to-night in the philosophical and fashionable circles on the Hill, while the Molineux people and the Gulls and the Fitz-Altamonts and the Sweenys all rode down to the caucus, to vote as Henry Gull, who managed the politics of the Hill, should direct them.

"And who are the Hill people going to send to the Board of Aldermen?" asked John Fisher, laughing at Harkness's lugubrious caricatures.

"Oh, they have got a fossil. Even you never heard of him, Mr. Fisher. They dug him up out of the graveyard. They have persuaded old Col. Stothers to run, and old Col. Stothers says, that, 'if a little of the sinews of war should prove necessary, he will venture to intimate that the fountain of the sinews will not soon run dry.' Old Col. Stothers is to take the stump against Michael Swinton! The caucus to-night will break up in a row. Swinton's people will adjourn to the Methodist vestry opposite, and you will have two tickets, and then Master Dick Mallory, the most popular and the most unreliable little son of perdition that ever lied to a woman or cheated a man, will slip into your City Council, over the head of both your candidates, and the good God only knows what mischief he will do when he gets there!"

This was poor Horace Harkness's peroration. He had occupied more time than his share in telling his story, and he knew he had. But all men knew the importance of it. Harkness had been spending all that day, all of many days, on this business. There was no one "of any account" in the Ward whom he had not seen about it. He had even talked suavely and with dignity with Col. Stothers. "I tell you" said Harkness, "I put on my dogskin gloves, I took a Malacca joint. I had Withers send a coupé to carry me, and we put Bob Sykes into livery for the occasion." But the Colonel's heart had not melted. Harkness seemed to have done all that a prudent and conciliatory counsellor could do. But the English of it all was that the Ward was fatally divided, and that at the very outset we had lost our best advantage. Worst of all, as it always is, we were sorest wounded in the house of our friends.

In such fashion we rapidly went round the semi-circle, and in longer or shorter reports obtained an interior view of the prospects of the great election from each of the twelve wards. There was never the slightest self-deception among these men. They spoke as clearly and calmly of defection or of accession to the forces of order, as a physician in consultation might speak of the temperature revealed by his thermometer, or the rapidity of the pulse as he had counted it. However pitilessly they might one day choose to brag before the public, there was no such bragging here. Some of the reports were encouraging; some seemed fatal. It was taken for granted that unless "*We*" carried eight wards handsomely, "*It*" scored a substantial victory. No one spoke of the parties in contest by any political or local names. It was "*We*" or "*They*," or, as I have written, "*We*" or "*It.*" They all understood entirely that their enemy moved as one man, and their whole object was to secure a concentration which might, in the least degree, rival a union so certain and so formidable.

How far they would succeed in this, I was by no means certain. "Where bad men conspire, good men must combine," Mr. Burke says, but he does not say, anywhere, how they are to do it. Cousin says, on the other hand, that low down in the quality of evil is its powerlessness, its incapacity to reproduce itself. This also is true.

But we were not worried about the evil of ten years to come. It was the evil of that autumn that we were in battle with. And that living Evil had power enough to do a great deal of harm in Tamworth, if it were permitted to take possession of the government now. How were you going to combine? You had twenty different corps and as many as five hundred corps commanders, and each corps commander had a special evil he wanted to crush and a special policy he wanted to carry out.

Indeed, I was reminded of Spain, where, with sixteen million people, they have sixteen million and one political parties.

But in John Fisher's library there was harmony, if only from that library it might take possession of the city, and the real leaders of the city.

Everybody knew that there were leaders; nobody complained of this. The opinions of the leaders had been obtained. Indeed, you might say that this meeting was meant chiefly for a report of what the leaders of the different shops, clubs, reading-rooms, unions, associations, corporations and companies, thought best and could stand by.

What they thought BEST, that was really the object which these twelve gentlemen who were "combining" with John Fisher believed was attainable, and indeed they thought it was the only thing worth fighting for. I was fairly awed sometimes by the cool puritanism with which some John Brown would make a report as to the tone of feeling of a knot of boys, hardly yet men, in a skating-rink which he seemed to be interested in. I was tempted to ask him if they did not open the rink with prayer. I am sure they might have done so, as he described the young fellows there, and have done it reverently.

When I did speak to him, he said, with a smile like Cromwell's, "We do not mean to let the Devil have all the fun."

The reports from the twelve wards were all made. John Fisher "résuméd" the position with wonderful clearness, and threw light on it, with a way to give every one courage. He then made two or three practical suggestions which led to discussion, and asked some questions which called forth answers. Of the result of the discussions this story will tell. I will not try to make the reader understand the detail.

Everything had to be considered. The people of the Causeway, justly irritated about the vote on their school-houses ; the whole interest of the Wire men, who had lost their water power when the canal was closed by the State, and had never had justice done them ; the evident unpopularity of the commission which was cutting down all the trees in the streets and substituting jonquils, with the best possible motives, but in face of public opinion ; the demands of the cabmen ; the rights of the street railways ; the need of the athletic clubs, who wanted new privileges in the park ; the failure of skating, now for two years,—all these interests and a hundred more, I suppose, were to be considered and conciliated. And IT was not to be permitted to handle one of them. Every one knew how IT manages such affairs.

For me, I listened longer than I understood, and when the company broke up into groups again, and different gentlemen began impressing their wishes on each other, I left the library and crossed to the parlor, where I hoped to find my guardian genius in the house, my " guide, philosopher and friend," Mary Bell.

I found there, as I knew I should, several ladies, generally the wives of the gentlemen who had met in the library. There was quite a little party assembled.

I joined Miss Bell at once.

It is very hard to describe the charm which this young woman,—I had almost said this girl,—already had over me. It is very hard to describe her. I have never known any one say she was beautiful when he had seen her but once ; nay, when he had only seen her, as you might see her, as she rode by in a carriage. On the other hand, if an impious person should say in a group of her friends that

Mary Bell is not beautiful, he would hardly escape with his life, after the assertion. Clearly the charm is in her expression, as people say, if they only quite knew what they meant. I have found this out, that her voice is very sweet, and shows its sweetness in talk quite as well and as often as in the elaborations of music.

What I said of her raving, when we were in the carriage, shows what is her enthusiasm for nature. Indeed, when I joined the party in the drawing-room, Mary Bell was saying to a Mr. Rossiter, who had left the library a little before me,

" Oh, yes! in the perfect world,—whenever we come so far,—all our dances will be out-of-doors."

They had been talking of the impromptu frolic, led by Mrs. Grattan, on the lawn.

" Then we shall certainly not dance much in what is now the dancing season," said he. " Low dresses and satin slippers will have little chance with the snow fifteen inches deep and the thermometer below zero."

" Who said satin slippers, Mr. Rossiter?" said she. " And who asked for low dresses? You only show your crass conservatism, as Mr. Mellen here would say. Only yesterday Mrs. Fisher brought home a charming book of national costumes, where there is a lovely Polish lady waltzing in fur boots and in a coat of furs.

" You may be sure that half the social evils you gentlemen are battling about in the library, come from the people's staying in-doors so much."

" I should like to know what you would say, after a winter with the Sioux on the plains," said he.

" Well, we need not push things to the extremes," said Mary Bell. " Perhaps the Sioux and we can meet half way. Let us persuade Stilling & Hausbilder to send them out a little consignment of frame houses—say ten thousand; that is nothing to Stilling & Hausbilder. That will make fifty thousand poor, freezing wretches comfortable. Then the Sioux may send back to me, and other long-suffering people like me, fifty thousand skins of ermine, and otter, and beaver, and elk, and bear, and we will be grateful to them, if only they or any power can keep us in the open air four hours of every winter day."

Mr. Rossiter laughed, and said that she solved the Indian problem very easily. She threw the solution, he observed, quite largely on Stilling & Hausbilder.

"Not too largely, perhaps," said Mary Bell, speaking now more seriously. "I do not know Mr. Stilling, but I do know Mr. Hausbilder. He helped me through so well with one of my poor people. A man who has worked his way up, every inch from the bottom. He knows what it is to be hungry, and what it is to be cold. And he is a man who takes hold with a will when there is anything to do.

"Yes; there are rich men, and rich men. Some of them, and this is one of them, like to succeed in their business. Just as Cordelia Grattan likes to write a good story; just as Meissonier likes to paint a good picture; just as Dr. Thorndike likes to have a patient get well, this Mr. Hausbilder likes to send a house to the king of the Cannibal Islands. He likes to have it go up without the sound of a hammer. He likes to imagine the king's satisfaction when he comes down from the hills after two days, and finds the house standing there. He likes to have anybody write and tell him about it.

"He does it because he likes it. He does not do it

because Mr. Ledger, the book-keeper, or Mr. Skinflint, the financial partner, tells him that they have made eleven hundred and twelve dollars and twenty-three cents on the houses they sent to the Cannibal Islands.

" He wants to have the people in this world live in better houses. This is his way of making the Kingdom of God come."

I said with some of her enthusiasm that Westerly said the same thing to me about clothing every twentieth man in the country. He took real pleasure, substantial pleasure, in knowing that they had better clothes on their backs than they would have had if he had not lived.

" No! " said Mary Bell. " I used to think the money part was the hard part. I do not think so now. Is not your poor Secretary of the Treasury half crazy because he does not know what to do with his money? He pulls down his vaults and builds larger.

" Poor man ! " and she shuddered. " I should think he would be so afraid of the parable."

Mr. Rossiter said that his mother used to say that she had been tried with all the trials except one. She was seventy years old, and said she wished she could be tried by Prosperity. She wanted to know how she should bear that.

" I wish I had known your mother," cried Mary Bell, and I saw that at the moment the young man's cheeks flushed red. He was not wholly under his own control. " I think," said she, " that I should have agreed with her in so many things."

Was Mr. Rossiter, then, so intimate with Miss Bell that she knew what his mother said or thought often?

She turned to me, and asked some question about what she called the caucus in the library.

I answered as well as I could. But I found I was annoyed, when Rossiter, who knew everybody and understood the lay of the land so much better than I did, was able to supplement my explanation, and, in fact, filled in the exact gap where mine failed.

Why was I annoyed? Mr. Rossiter did this without the least presumption or affectation. Why should he not tell Miss Bell what she wanted to know?

None the less I was annoyed, and I was annoyed because I was annoyed. Who was this Mr. Rossiter? I crossed the room to ask my other friend in the family, Cordelia Grattan, who was just leaving the piano.

But at this moment there was a general incursion of all the men in the library. We had but few ladies in the drawing-room to meet the requisitions, or to make agreeableness, light and sweetness for so great a multitude, still, our little handful of skirmishers formed in open order to receive infantry as well as they could.

But Cordelia Grattan was surrounded by half-a-dozen gentlemen beside myself, and I found I had no chance to ask her personal questions about the company.

CHAPTER IX.

I MUST not attempt to follow, in such detail, the successive days of even the short visit which I made with John Fisher. To the last, each day was a day of surprises. I never knew whether we were to be artists, or historians, or people of fashion, or ecclesiastics, or patrons of education. Days came, indeed, when we led a simple home life, if we chose, though there was always a good deal of coming and going for those who would. The children were bright, wide-awake, intelligent girls and boys, who were evidently made to understand that they must take their share in the work of the world, and not expect play unmixed with work, or sugar without its share of lemon-juice.

I was very much interested to see how John Fisher made both boys and girls his companions. They were as much at home in his work-room as he was. Those who were old enough would copy a letter, or translate an invoice, as if they had been trained clerks. And, in talk at table, he took it for granted that they were interested in what interested him, as if indeed they had been his partners.

There were horses and carriages enough in the stables to meet the requisitions even of the most varied caprice. And people used them freely. I had been driving one morning, early in my visit, with Mrs. Grattan. I had tried to draw out from her some hints as to the standing and influence of one or two of the gentlemen with whom I had affairs in the city, and not without success. But I may as well confess that my secret object in proposing the drive had been to come at some better understanding about Mary Bell and her position in the family. Mary Bell lent a hand always, but she did not seem like what one calls a "German wife," that convenient member in a large German household who relieves the lady of the house from all care, and leaves her free for all relaxation and amusement. Yet she did not seem to me on a visit simply, as I was. Servants and children seemed to recognize her presence as if she were to the manor bred, and was to remain there. There had been no talk of her arrival, and there was no allusion to her going away.

I quite pleased myself with my skill in leading up to talk of Miss Bell, as if I had not led up to it. And very much was I pleased by Mrs. Grattan's frank and hearty enthusiasm about her. I had seen, before this, the simple and wholly unconscious way in which a lady of large fortune can speak of some old school friend, who is living on three hundred a year, as if income were of no consequence, and a few millions in bonds, more or less, a sheer nothing, in comparison with good temper, or pleasant memories of school. Cordelia Grattan spoke now in this easy way; she spoke with all the eagerness of a determined friend, and, what pleased me most, she recognized the absolutely indescribable charm in Mary Bell, which had so attracted me, and which I found it impossible to define.

I did not, however, dare talk too long, even on a subject so agreeable. As if we had come on it merely by chance, sure that I could now renew it when I would, I put in an allusion to Mrs. Fisher, who confused me more and more. And once more, just as it had been with Miss Bell, once or twice, when I had tried such an experiment, I was landed in Antipodes.

"I thought Mrs. Fisher seemed annoyed this morning when the children spoke of Dr. Lemon's lecture. Is she so fond of him?" This was my ingenious question.

"I think you did not hear Dr. Lemon." This was the more ingenious reply. For the subtle lady went on, "You must not pretend to talk of the Philippine Islands, until you have heard all our missionary course. We shall teach you the difference between Apiu and Opiana. That is really a curious business, the traces of taboo after two generations of Christianity. Did you——" etc., etc., etc., and not one word, too, from me as to Mrs. Fisher or her peculiarities.

As we drove up to the door my lively companion looked at her watch, and declared that we were late, and that she had to dress. "And we must be very early," she said "for the ministers will only adjourn for an hour. They will call it an hour, and in truth it will be only an hour and a half."

"Ministers!" said I, amazed. For I had thought we were to lunch by ourselves.

"Is it possible," said she, as she jumped from the carriage, "that you are so taken up with your licenses and your drunkenness that you do not know that the Convention of Covenanters met here this morning? Why all the chiefs, the presiding elders and all the rest are to lunch with us, and I must run up stairs to attend to my finery."

CHAPTER X.

ONE of the servants confirmed Mrs. Grattan's statement. Lunch was to be served half an hour earlier than usual.

The second secession of Reformed Covenanters holds very much the same position in Tamworth which the Greek church has in Moscow, the Latin church in Rome, the English church in Canterbury, and your own church, dear reader, in the particular city or town in which you read these lines.

Possibly it might fare as well without a Decennial Convention as with one. But its leaders do not think so, and on this occasion one of these great historical gatherings came in on us just as we were preparing for our critical local election.

Some two thousand delegates were in town, quartered by a central committee on the different residents, and I soon found that eight or ten of them had been billeted on Mr. Fisher, and were beginning their visit under our hospitable roof. Some forty or fifty others had been asked to-day to lunch, and had accepted under the stern condition that they could be only absent from the town hall an hour, or, at the most, an hour and a half. On such occasions the clergy are regardless of dyspepsia, as indeed they are, perhaps, on too many others.

I had scarcely entered the parlors where they met, when I saw that John Fisher's invitations had been wisely given, whoever had been trusted with that affair. Wisely, I mean, if he meant to have the leaders of opinion, or those who thought they were. For, though there were sitting meekly by different doors, in small chairs, with their backs to the wall, two or three of those timid brethren who always make one element of such a party and take this method of giving literal obedience to the instructions of the parable, the large part of the company were men at ease in society, men who would have attracted note anywhere, and were not unused to offering their opinions, and commanding respect for them. They were in half-a-dozen groups, eagerly discussing the policies of the convention, past and to come. There was the inevitable group of those who wanted the "business" to go on in a pre-ordained and well-regulated fashion. There was the other inevitable group of those who considered that this well-regulated fashion had been regulated only by Satan, or one of his satellites, and who were determined to overthrow it. But these different groups were perfectly good-tempered; and, from one nebula to another, messenger comets passed, from time to time, bringing or carrying one or another proposition for conciliation. "Would White accept such an amendment?" or, "Would Jones withdraw his motion till Brown had offered his?" or, "Would Black yield the floor to Gray, that Gray might explain White's amendment to Black?" All this was eagerly canvassed while we waited the short summons to what was called "lunch," and was an elaborate dinner.

Be it known to readers in Europe that the hospitality of the great Western cities of America does not limit itself severely by names. You are asked to dine at six, and you decline because you are engaged elsewhere. Then you are asked to lunch at one, and you accept, and the provision made for you is perhaps identical in form with what it would be at the most elaborate dinner. At least it is such as would have been ample for Amadis, were he looking on food for the last time before a six days' encounter with giants.

I sat at Mrs. Fisher's end of one of two long tables which had been set in the largest drawing-room of the house, the ample dining-room even being insufficient for so large a company. I found, as I had expected, that all the more prominent of the clergy of the neighborhood were there, of whatever communion. There were two bishops, for instance, and all the professors of both theological schools. On this occasion all warfare between "Homoi" and "Homo" ceased, and there was no difference between an ultra Montanist and an Ultra-montanist. On other days the hyphen separates two worlds of belief. We were the lions and the lambs, and while we discussed the oysters, the clear soup, the white fish, the fillet and other necessaries of life at Mr. Fisher's board, we did not feast upon each other.

But I need hardly say that Mrs. Fisher did her best to disturb this harmony. Nothing but the admirable breeding of the different theologians prevented her. I hardly ought, however, to give her credit for any intention in the matter. I think that she simply gabbled from "native impulse, elemental force," as a forgotten poet says. None the less it is true, as Henry Kingsley says, that, when the Devil has no knave for an errand, he sends a fool, and that this answers quite as well.

My experience has confirmed Henry Kingsley's. Mrs. Fisher, of course, did not know the names of many of the strangers. But she did know the clergymen of Tamworth, and perhaps had herself arranged that most of these gentlemen should sit at our end of her table. So soon as there was a chance, she began with her little compliments.

"My dear Professor Prince, let me thank you with all my heart for your charming article in the *Panoplist*. I would not go to bed till I had read it through. I said to Cordelia, ' You may go to bed, the rest of you, but I will read every word of this paper ; it is so convincing and cogent.' And so instructive, too ! I agree with you in every word, and I know my husband does. Do not you, Dr. Witherspoon? Have you seen the *Panoplist ?*"

Now the truth was that it was only by the merest accident that Mrs. Fisher knew that there was any such article. She had happened to see the magazine on the library table on that morning, and had observed Professor Prince's name, as one of the authors, on the cover. Unfortunately, too, the article was a bitter personal attack on this very Dr. Wither-spoon to whom she appealed so confidently. It was, indeed, much more sharp than are even the terms of ordinary "theological hatred"; and I fancy that even Prince himself was thoroughly ashamed of it by this time.

But Dr. Witherspoon is a well-bred man, and was equal to the emergency.

"I have not read my *Panoplist* carefully," said he; "I opened on their article on the 'Lost Cities of Edom,' and that sent me back to Waddington's book, which I had not seen. Mr Alvord," he added, bowing to one of the strange gentlemen, "I think you have been in Edom?"

And they launched at once into questions of trans-Jordanic antiquities, quite to Mrs. Fisher's amazement. She had heard of "lost cities," and had practiced a little in the game which bears that name. You hide the name of Troy, for instance, in such a phrase as "What royal weather." Mrs. Fisher tried to recollect how the word "Elyria" was buried in the phrase, "John's grandmother died yesterday." But she had either confounded the name "Elyria" with some other name, or it was not John's grandmother who had died. Poor Dr. Lemon had never heard of the game, and did not in the least understand what she meant. While he listened to her he was trying to catch what the traveler said, and he put in "Yes" and "No," and "That is curious," in very bad places. But Mrs. Fisher did not mind this; and Professor Prince seemed to me ashamed of his ill-nature, and glad for the relief Mr. Alvord gave him.

Mrs. Fisher had lately returned from a six weeks' visit in

Baltimore, and some one asked her if there had not been an
unusual religious interest there. "Oh, yes! I think so;
I know there was; Mrs. Carrol was speaking to Miss Linders
about it, I am quite sure, the morning we drove in the park.
But you know I had such a cold all the time I was in Baltimore." Poor Dr. Lemon on one side of her, and Dr. Vanderweyer on the other, had to give her up at last. But she
would not give them up. Lemon was perfectly delighted to
find himself so near the great Dr. Vanderweyer. Vanderweyer was just home from traveling in Europe. He had
dined with Gladstone; Ruskin had taken him through the
galleries; he had even traveled with Tennyson, had met
Martineau and Cardinal Wiseman again and again; had been
made a guest and was quite at home at Balliol, and in Paris
had been invited to lecture. It was a great thing for quiet Dr.
Lemon to meet Vanderweyer, and hear him talk. He would
not talk across Mrs. Fisher, but he did think he might pick
up some crumbs. He was doomed to disappointment.

After the episode with Professor Prince, she turned to her
neighbor and said to him, "Doctor, I have been dying
to see your wife, and now I shall send her a message by
you."

"Yes," said the great man, and he added gallantly that he
would not forget one message though she should give him
one hundred. What could Mrs. Vanderweyer write or do?
He should be at home on Monday, and Mrs. Fisher should
hear directly.

"I want her to send me word, Doctor, whether she puts
camphor under the edges of her carpets, or whether she ever
tried green tobacco leaves. I read in a newspaper that crude
camphor," etc., etc., etc.

And this ended all hope of hearing any of the central axioms of life from Dr. Vanderweyer.

The courses were very promptly served. The ministers seemed to be men not unused to eating rapidly, and talking a good deal at the same time. Within an hour and twenty minutes, this little interlude to the great discussions of the convention was over; and Fisher and his wife, Mrs. Grattan, Miss Bell and I, found ourselves alone in the library.

" Peace after storm," said Mary Bell.

"Storm!" said Fisher, laughing. "We had no storm at our end of the table. They were as good-natured as lambs."

"My gentlemen were good-natured enough," said she. "But they forgot my existence. There was so much talk about the amendment, and the rider, and the original proposition and the substitute, that I really forgot minor matters, as the Ten Commandments and Beatitudes. I wonder if I did not steal that little man's handkerchief," and she pretended to look at her own to see what initials were marked on it.

"But that is the manner of conventions," said our good-natured host. " Think what a variety this is to these gentlemen. Those very neighbors of yours, now; for six months, those good fellows have had no chance to try their hand in governing in this fashion. One of them has been begging money for Siloam college; one of them has been bullying the school committee of Cranberry Centre; one of them has fought through his drainage scheme for Hollybank, and that little white one had been reading his proof-sheets for a new translation of the ' Wisdom of the Son of Sirach.' It does them no end of good to be shaken up together. The ministers' parties are the most interesting to me of all of them. Because, if you ask the right men, any forty of them take a wider range than any other forty men you can light on easily."

I said I did not see that.

" Oh !" said Fisher. "Forty artists all talk Rose Madder and wrinkled canvas.

"Forty newspaper men all talk about the Associated Press.

"Forty authors talk about International Copyright.

"But you get forty ministers together, and you do not know what will come. They will talk about anything in the heavens above or the earth beneath."

" What I know, " said Mrs. Fisher, " is that that ridiculous Mr. Alvord does not know what a lost city is."

Fisher took me off with him.

" It is a good thing," he said, "to bring the different kinds together. At heart, the ministers themselves are catholic and tolerant. It is rather the denominational newspapers which keep up the sectarianism of the country. The ministers themselves know they are in the same boat, and, whenever they are thrown together, they find a thousand ways to help each other."

CHAPTER XI.

WHEN the carriage came for me, which my friends of the Temperance Society had sent, on the evening of my speech, I noticed that there was a policeman on the box with the coachman. I had been, I confess, a little disappointed when I found that Mrs. Grattan and Miss Bell were not coming to the meeting. John Fisher did join me.

The two members of the committee who escorted us were gentlemen I had not met before, and, at the very first, I fancied that they were more excited than the occasion seemed to me to warrant. Scarcely were we in the carriage when one of them began to advise the coachman as to his route.

" Careful Thomas ; be sure you turn in by Ninth street. Don't let them see you on the avenue."

Then the other tried to soothe him. " You are nervous, Harry ; you are nervous. You've never been under fire." But, though he said to me, in a reassuring way," It is all right ; it is all right, Mr. Mellen," it was clear enough to me that he was the more nervous of the two.

Gradually it leaked out that a row was quite probable. All the afternoon handbills had been circulated, and posters on the walls had announced that no Chinaman should speak in Tamworth. Some ingenious liquor dealer, who had wanted to break up the meeting, had given the idea that, because I had just come from San Francisco, I was an apostle of Chinese labor, of the religion of Confucius in general and particular. When our friends had left the hall, to come for us, a considerable crowd was already around the doors, and one of them had heard an address in which it was explained that Chinamen ate rats, and could therefore under-bid the regular workman in his own market. It had also been explained that he drank nothing but bilge-water, and, as soon as he arrived, would prohibit the sale of whisky and lager. The keeper of the hall had shown the white feather, and wanted to postpone the meeting. But bolder counsels had prevailed. He had been compelled to light up, and had been bidden to open the doors at the usual hour. The Mayor had been notified of the danger, and now our carriage was to dodge through the streets, that I might enter quietly at the back of the hall through Judge Tristum's private door.

This was the reason why John Fisher had bidden Miss Bell and Mrs. Grattan stay away. I say "bidden"; he advised at first, and they were only more eager to be present. He had been forced to assume for once the aspect of command.

As for his wife, he knew she would not come, because as late as dinner she had said she should certainly be one of the party.

We made the transit safely through Judge Tristum's office. The old gentleman was there himself, with both his sons, to join us on the platform. "It is a good while since I have gone to a temperance meeting, Mr. Mellen," he said to me. "But this promises to be interesting," with a delightful smile. Then we were both introduced to Mr. Stepney, a young man whom I had never met, who was to make the first speech. He looked to me a little pale. But I found I misjudged him, if I thought him afraid.

The moment we were on the platform there was no question as to what would be the experience of the evening, had there, indeed, been any room for question before.

As we crossed to our seats we could see that the hall was crowded, every seat filled, and the aisles between jammed close with such a host of men as one never saw at a temperance meeting before. Every now and then a bottle would be tossed from one side to another, caught, and a pretence made of drinking. As we entered a shout rose of "No rats! No rats!" and one boy cried out, "Where's the rat-catcher?" by which epithet I know he meant me.

Had they but known it, it so happens that I sympathize

through and through with the feeling on the Pacific coast, that our civilization is our own, and that we ought not to be expected to receive all the overplus of Asia. I know that, if I lived there, I should join in very stringent measures, so they were legal, to keep out the Chinaman. I never forgot how Arinori, the Japanese minister, once said to me, "If I were an American statesman, I would resist the Chinese invasion with the last drop of my blood." But the platform and the meeting were no place for me to say this. I saw in a minute that this crowd was of that complexion and quality which, as Curran says, "It is not well to run away from." I altered the plan of my speech a little, that it should be sufficiently defiant, and waited the issue.

The meeting was opened in form, and little Stepney sailed in magnificently. If the little fellow was frightened, he did not show it more than Hardy did when he led the English line at Trafalgar. Hardly had he begun when a dead rat, thrown from the floor, grazed his ear and struck the wall behind. But, on the same instant, a stout policeman collared the boy who threw the rat, lifted him from his place and passed him, over the heads of some orderly people in front, to three or four other officers, who huddled him out by a side door. Meanwhile cries from the hall, "Let him alone! This is not the Chinaman! Down in front! Let him go on!" with appeals from the chairman, finally subsided into a calm, and Stepney got a chance to put in a hundred words extremely well. Since than I have marked him as an orator. The true orator is he who knows how to place his first hundred words.

He made a ringing and effective speech to an audience, half of whom had never heard such a speech before. He had won their attention in that first minute and he never lost it. They fairly applauded him when he sat down.

But I, who was to follow, did not deceive myself for a moment. I had had the chance which Stepney gave me, by speaking a full half-hour, to recast my speech. I saw that full half my audience were well disposed, or, rather, were so disposed that they wanted nothing better than a fight in which they might turn these rowdies out-of-doors. The episode of the boy, captured and "jugged," showed that law and order had a certain power in the hall. None the less, however, was it clear that I must take and keep an attitude of confidence, even of attack.

I was met as I stepped forward with ringing cheers and howls of derision. I bowed to the cheers, waited for them to stop, nodded to one and another friend, and then waved my hand as if they were all my friends. By this sheer audacity I won silence. When it was perfect silence I began:

"Have you no good liquor in Tamworth? And what do you pay for it? I saw a man on Fourth street selling poor Indiana wish-wash at ten cents a drink' yesterday. Do you stand that? That man bought at a dollar and ten cents a gallon, and sold for six dollars a gallon. We know better than that in our country."

The sheer surprise of the audience at such secular remarks from a "distinguished" Temperance orator, as the bills and the president had described me, gave me the all-essential five minutes, by the loss of which any speech is lost, and by the winning of which, probably, any speech is saved. All the beginning of the address was a subtle attack on the retailers (who were, in fact, ruining half my audience), and was what, I dare say, the men among them were in the habit of saying

to each other, when they had a chance to look back and see
where their money had gone to.   I passed to more dangerous
ground.   "Why should Jem Vilas and Tom Sayers want to
keep their shops open on Sunday, when I may not sell dry
goods; when Mr. Fisher may not make machinery; when the
trains may not run on Sunday?"   If a man bought fruit and
had it Saturday night, it might rot in the shop before Monday
morning, and the law would not let him sell it.   Why should
the law be more mild on McGullian and on Harris, than it
was on Warder or Trott, who sold strawberries and bananas?

But by this I was losing sympathy.   This whole row had
been created by half-a-dozen men who had been fined once and
again for selling liquors on Sunday.   They were in presence
before me, with a dozen of their bar-tenders, and hundreds of
their customers.   I was very soon warned by a rotten egg, full
on the bosom of my shirt, that there were some good pitchers
in the gallery, and, at the moment when this struck me, a
voice from the gallery cried out, "Tell us how to cook rats!
Turn him round; we want to see his tail!" and my periods
were lost in howls; in screams; in cross-talking—all resulting
in that chaos confounded, which takes possession of a great
hall when a thousand people are all expressing their senti-
ments together.   A somewhat noisy sergeant of police made
himself rather conspicuous.   But, really, he was powerless.
The hall was too full for any person to move from place to
place without the ready help of those among whom he moved.
To make an arrest and carry off the victim was simply
impossible.

While this chaos lasted, I stood talking with Fisher and
the president of the evening.   After ten minutes, more or less,
I stepped forward again, waved my hand as before, and as

before commanded instant silence; for if every man stops talking, by surprise, the place is as silent as creation was in the beginning.

"Let me tell you," I said, "how we do in China!"

The audacity of this speech saved it as before.

"The men give their money Saturday night to their wives. I know a woman who made her husband promise to buy all his liquor of her, and she would only get what he liked. She got old Bourbon, Dry-mash, and three or four more of the best Kentucky brands. She made her parlor into a pretty drinking-place, she got a neighbor to teach her how to mix liquors well, and made it very pleasant for her husband and his friends. He liked her shop better than anybody's. It was the prettiest shop in town. She could buy at wholesale of the big dealers, who ride in carriages, and have plenty of money. And her husband, instead of drinking once a day, drank three times a day, and then he drank five times in a day, and, the more he drank, the more money she made. And at last he died in the horrors. And she had saved up money enough, in the five years she had been killing him, to build herself a cottage on the hill and to send all the children to the Academy."

I had taken them again by surprise, and a parable is always listened to. People will remember a parable fifty years, when they do not remember an argument for an hour. Also, we gained a laugh; a hearty laugh from the audience, and a laugh is a great thing on the side of order. I had no passion for speech under the circumstances. I thought if I could close handsomely, without one more storm, we should come off with the honors. One does not seek much logical connection in such surroundings. Indeed,

it is a fault in any public address, to a general audience, to
be very careful to tell why you say what you say. Say it.
That is the best rule.

"What reason is there why a handful of ten men should
govern Tamworth? What makes Harry Redmond a better
man than my friend, yonder, who threw the turnip at me?
Why is Fritz Reidelberger more fit to govern Tamworth
than Rudolph Kramer or Carl Schmidt? Who told Frank
Wallis that he was one of the rulers of Tamworth to rule you
workingmen, who held the votes of Tamworth——" And,
by this time, they saw I was reading from a list, on which
were Redmond's name, Reidelberger's and Wallis's. I went
through the list of ten. "These are the ten men whose
names are on all the bonds of all the liquor-dealers here.
There is not a poor man who wants to sell you or me whisky
but he has had to go to one of these men and make a bow to
him, and ask him to sign his license bond. These ten men it is,
who mean to tell you how to vote when the Election Day
comes round. These ten men will meet in the private office
of somebody's brewery——"

"Fitting place!" screamed an enthusiast, delighted to have
a few bottom facts alluded to.

"I do not know your names," said I, "only I took this
list yesterday from the Registrar's office. These ten men
will meet somewhere, and they will make the list of votes
which you are to carry when that day comes round.

"Now, you are Americans, all of you. You do not mean
to be led by the nose! If these men were priests, and had
their heads shaven, and wore long black coats, with little
whole white collars round their necks, and they came and
told you how to vote, you would pack them all on a train

and send them to the place they came from. If they
were in any uniform, if they wore red coats, or if they
had silver buttons on their sleeves, like the Greasers yonder
in Mexico, you would heat a tar-barrel and give them a
coat of white feathers. But they do not wear uniforms.
They only act uniform. They do not show their colors.
They meet in the back parlor, and the ticket——"

This was as far as I ever went in that speech. By this
time the men who had undertaken to capture the meeting
had quite enough of it and of me. They were on their
feet again, howling. The men behind them were howling
again in one interest or another. Such missiles as remained
were flung upon the stage. Stepney made a clever diversion
by catching a cabbage, as if it had been a base-ball, and
tossing it across to the President. But at this moment a
critical accident ended the whole thing. Some one slung a
heavy rutabaga at me. It missed me, but struck John
Fisher rather heavily, as he sat at my left. It scratched
his cheek and drew blood, which flowed rapidly, so that in a
moment his collar was red and the wristband of his sleeve,
where he had held his hand to the wound. At the moment,
one saw the regard which the real people had for this quiet
man. He had refused to speak; not a word would he say.
But that stain of a few drops of blood was more eloquent
than any words. "Shame! Shame!" cried some Stentor.
"Shame! Shame!" echoed all the well-meaning men in the
hall. They had now a cry, a symbol, and a purpose. They
rose to their feet. They collared and dragged off one and
another of the rioters. The fussy sergeant threw open some
great escape doors which were made for fires. The noisy
part of the assembly, those who were not yet in the grasp of

anybody, thought best to disappear. And in five minutes
the great hall was nearly empty.   On the platform, we were
well satisfied to see that nobody was really hurt, and in the
excitement of the moment we all agreed that things had
turned better than we had feared.

I took the whole thing to heart, as showing, as I had not
guessed before, how simply a man might make himself, and
deserve to be, really an idol of the people.

CHAPTER XII.

[INTERPOLATED IN MR. MELLEN'S MEMOIRS.]

THE adventure at the Temperance meeting, in which Mr.
Mellen played a part so important, made him, naturally
enough, quite a hero in the life of Tamworth, for a few days,
and especially in the house of John Fisher.   Mrs. Fisher
had gone comfortably to bed before the gentlemen came
home ; nor did she inquire or hear anything of their conflicts
until morning.   Then she was quite sure that she had expected all that had passed, and had warned every one that it
would happen, just as it had happened, She said it was
always so, and that her advice was always rejected.   She
also said that if she had had the slightest idea that there
would have been any danger, she should have ordered her
own carriage and should have bidden Barney drive her
through the crowd to the front of the entrance of the hall,

where she should have herself addressed the people. And she gave what the reporters would have called a sketch of her address. She also said that if they had not stolen away as they did, she should have insisted on going with them to the hall, that they could have entered early and taken their seats on the platform before the mob arrived ; and she sketched another speech, which she would have delivered before the meeting, and which would have prevented all the difficulties which followed. At different periods in the narrative at breakfast, she offered other suggestions equally consistent, and equally confused. They threw Mr. Mellen out a little, and he found it rather difficult to meet them. But all the others seemed to understand that all this was "pretty Fanny's way," and to take them for granted, without reply or comment.

So far was Mrs. Fisher justified in complaining, as she always did, that nobody paid any attention to any of her suggestions.

Mrs. Grattan and Mary Bell were both up and eagerly waiting for the returning party. John Fisher and his friend told the story, in varied interruptions, both of them, of course, a good deal excited. Mr. Mellen stood this supreme test very well. He had really kept his temper through the whole scene, and had shown tact and spirit in playing with his persecutors. But he told his part of the tale modestly, and gave full credit to all the other actors on his side, particularly to little Stepney, who had sailed in so magnificently and had come out so well. But John Fisher did not mean to have his friend's light hid under any bushel. He gave him full credit for his pluck ; he let the ladies understand the full extent of the danger, and Mr. Mellen appeared in the most charming character of all, as a modest hero, while he ate the oyster soup and the omelette with herbs which the care of the housekeeper had provided.

" My dear Mrs. Edwards," John Fisher had said to that functionary, " people are always very hungry when they have been speaking to mobs."

The reader has perhaps suspected Mr. Mellen had not been thrown, day by day, with Mary Bell, as one who was largely under instructions in this Tamworth life, without himself feeling the force of the fascination to which once and again he alluded in his papers. It would be queer if he had not felt it. He had knocked about the world a good deal, and it is no business of this writer to tell what had been his experiences in the society of women before. But this the reader may be told, that he had never so far lost his heart but that he got it back again. He had never married, though he believed in marriage. He was, it may be added, generally liked by women ; he talked well with women, which means that he recognized their good sense and ability, and did not treat them like fools ; he had implicit faith in women, and held the highest standard as to what a woman might be and what she should not be. So high was this standard, indeed, that it seemed as if it had often been too high for the women whom he had measured by it. His life, too, had been to some extent a vagrant life, and he had not often had the chance to show to any really first-rate woman how much of a man he was. For some reason or other, in brief, when Mr. Mellen met Mary Bell, he was neither heart-touched anywhere else, nor engaged, nor married. A man may be heart-touched who is not engaged, and, alas ! a man who is not heart-touched may be engaged or may be married. But neither of these things could be said of Mr. Mellen.

Up to the event at the Temperance lecture, Mr. Mellen could never have thought that Mary Bell took any more interest in him than she might in any other guest in the house; or, indeed, than she showed for many of the other gentlemen who came in again and again in its profuse hospitality. Indeed, he had permitted himself to be annoyed, one evening, because Mr. Rossiter was so intimate with her, or because she permitted his intimacy.

But, on the morning after the " adventure," as they came to call it, Mr. Mellen found, and was naturally not displeased to find, that he was quite a hero with all the ladies. They wanted him to tell the story again. They read aloud the newspaper accounts of it, and compared them with each other. They tried to make him say he had not slept well, and, indeed, beset him with a hundred nameless attentions such as shall not be here described, but which are the fair reward of the brave. He was no fool. But he was not displeased at the good fortune which had given him such regard, where, in his heart, he knew he prized it most. He sat talking with them in the comfortable parlor, where every one liked to linger after breakfast, longer, much longer, than was usual. Then Mrs. Fisher bustled off, with some pretence as to something disagreeable which she was to do. Cordelia Grattan goodnaturedly took herself out of the way, and Mr. Mellen promptly followed up his opportunity by asking Miss Bell if she would not let him take her to drive. There had been some talk of a drive, that he might see the water-fall at Newry Gap.

" Drive, Mr. Mellen? Have you forgotten to-day's duties in your triumph for last night's success?"

"Duties!" said poor Mr. Mellen; "I had thought my duties were all done. I was asked to make a speech, and I have come and made it, as far as my audience would let me ; if, indeed, they may be called an audience, who were resolved not to listen.

"No, I ought really to go away, and be making speeches at Chicago, and at Dunleith, and at Cleveland, and at Turk's Hollow. But I am quite too much interested in your election, and I have told Fisher I should stay and see who is chosen Alderman from the Hill."

"Exactly," said she, "I heard you say so. And do you not put this and that together enough to see that the laying of the corner-stone has its part also in the election?"

"Corner-stone! What corner-stone?"

"Mr. Mellen, you will never understand Tamworth. Here I have been instructing you and instructing you, and you are so shut up with your prohibition and license that you do not so much as know that we lay the corner-stone for an Art Gallery to-day. Mr. Fisher is Chairman of the Trustees. Mrs. Dolliber and Mrs. Thurtle are a Committee of ladies to procure a silver trowel. Cordelia Grattan has written an ode, and Dr. Witherspoon is to deliver an oration ; and after all you ask me to go to ride, on that very day, to see a water-fall.

"This is your interest in politics."

"I did know," said he, rather ruefully, "that Mrs. Grattan had written an ode. I helped her with a line that was limping. I did know that Dr. Witherspoon was to ' pronounce,' as he said, an oration. But I should much prefer to go to drive with you. And as to all this taking place to-day, I have heard no time fixed, nor have I expected to. All that I know in this house is that they always do something, and that the something is always what you would not expect. It goes without saying, that it is different from the something of the day before."

" Be warned, then, in time. At noon you will meet at the Art Club ; in full dress, too, Mr. Mellen. And then a procession of you gentlemen will move, as the newspapers say, to the spot. There you will see Mrs. Grattan looking pale from anxiety, and you will not see me. I shall be hidden among the contraltos of the chorus of the Jubal."

Mr. Mellen declared that he should know her among nine hundred other contraltos. But this was the only word of gallantry or of tenderness he had any chance to thrust into the conversation. For, as she spoke, her hand was on the door.

It seemed but fair to give the reader a hint of what does not appear in his own language in his memoirs, that just at this time, when accident had made him a bit of a hero, Mr. Mellen made sure that Mary Bell was the noblest woman and the loveliest in the world, and determined to tell her so.

CHAPTER XIII.

[MR. MELLEN RESUMES.]

AFTER we had been sufficiently questioned, pitied. and praised, the morning after our Temperance conflict, it proved that all more agreeable and private enterprises must be set aside, for that day at least, while we laid the corner-stone of the "Academy of Fine Art." The establishment of this Academy, as I found out, had been a favorite enterprise now for a year or two in Tamworth, and all our household was committed. The corner-stone must be laid of course, for there could not be an Academy without a corner. And the affair was so important that the Mayor and Aldermen and all officials were to join. The school regiment was to parade, and a general holiday had been given. I found that even at the mills they would shut down at twelve o'clock for the day.

I was by no means sure whether my presence would add to the hilarity of the occasion. For it was quite certain that there were eggs and ruta-bagas left in Tamworth, and if any of my friends of last night's audience happened to recognize their target, and begin on another course of projectiles, it might be disagreeable to my neighbors, unless the marksmanship were better by day than by night. But no one else intimated any doubts as to my going; indeed, it seemed taken for granted that I should go. The ceremony would be long. We had an early lunch, and hurried down to be at the Athenæum Hall at noon. And I may as well say, now and here, that neither egg nor turnip disturbed the solemnities of the day. The rowdies of the night before took no interest in this occasion.

At the Athenæum Hall I found all the magnates of the town. The Mayor and Aldermen, and Common Council, and School Committee were there, ninety-nine different people chosen to executive business, in which they were to oversee the expenditure of three or four million dollars. A railway or a factory, with the same annual expense, would have been owned perhaps by a thousand people, but they would take care not to have more than four or five responsible directors.

This was the remark John Fisher made to me, as he

looked round to see which of the City Government I should best like to know.

I was amused to see that, literally, he knew every man in the room. He shook hands with every one, and called each correctly by name.

" We are in full force, Mr. Mayor," he said.

" Yes. Everybody is interested. Most of them think they are the founders of the Academy ; that is well."

" The more founders, the better, if they will not forget that founders must maintain. How does the fund stand?"

And then the Mayor, in rather a lower tone, began to tell him who had been written to, and who had answered. There was a son of the town who had lately had new views on religion, which had impelled him to go and establish a sheep walk in Montana, where his late father had a great silver mine. It had been hoped that, if he were " properly approached," he might contribute fifty thousand dollars to the fund for the Academy. But it was clear from the way in which the Mayor shook his head, and put his finger to his forehead, that he feared that this new Mahomet, on his sheep ranch, had not wits enough left to sign a check, even if " proper influence" could make him see the value of the Academy. There was a rich widow at Munich, preparing herself to paint portraits. She also had been " approached in the proper direction," but she had made no answer. Whether Mr. Lathers, the great lumber man, would subscribe, also seemed doubtful. If the Ranchman proved able to draw a check, it seemed certain that Lathers would wish to " go one better." But if the Ranchman's wits failed him at the critical moment, it was feared that Lathers would prove indifferent to Fine Art.

"In short," said John Fisher, "it is the old story, that nothing succeeds like success——"

"They are on time," cried a bright little man, whom I had seen flying about everywhere, and who was clearly a sort of Lord High Chamberlain on the occasion.

His real official position was that of Clerk of Committees ; his duty was to supply brains and etiquette both, to such persons among the ninety-nine governors of Tamworth, as, by any accident, found themselves destitute of either. As he spoke, he pointed out of the window, where a light column of steam showed that the lightning express was at that moment passing the viaduct at Kroom's Hollow. On the lightning express were the Governor and staff, who were to make a part of the ceremonial of the day. In fact, as I afterwards found, the Governor was another person who thought he was the inventor and founder of the Academy. The Superintendent of Education, who came with him, knew that he himself was. The truth was, that a quiet little Mr. Mole, a second cousin of the Count of that name, who fought Louis Napoleon, had conceived the whole plan. He came on in the legislative train, and as the "exercises" went on, I had a good deal of very satisfactory talk with him. He and John Fisher were almost the only men in the company who made no public addresses on the occasion.

Ten minutes more were enough to bring the lightning express into the station, to transfer the Governor and suite into their carriages, and to bring them to us ; for there had been no guard of honor at the platform, nor any presenting arms. The Governor, in his turn, was introduced to all of the Aldermen and to the members of the Committee of Reception, all of whom wore sashes of pale blue silk. The

Lieutenant Governor and the military gentlemen of the staff were also introduced. The Governor was asked if he would have a little Orange-Phosphate, and he and the other gentlemen accepted. They had traveled two hundred and seventy miles since they breakfasted, but it seemed to be understood that they were quite ready for this laborious day, without other refreshment. They did not themselves make any difficulty about this.

Accordingly, in a few minutes more, the little Clerk of Committees announced that all was ready. The Governor led by the Mayor, the Lieutenant Governor led by the President of the Aldermen, and others with fit escort, filed out of the hall, and we gathered on the elegant portico of the building. In front was the school regiment, of a thousand or more boys. So soon as the Governor appeared, they presented arms, and they stood at " present " while the rest of the procession arranged itself. Mr. Mole and I were, as " invited guests," near enough to the Governor to hear his compliment to the Mayor.

" I could hardly have given you such an escort for a ceremony, Mr. Mayor, without a ' special act' ; at least, I should have to send over half the State for so many companies."

" We were laughing about that," said the Mayor. " If the President were here he has under his orders in this State one one-legged sergeant at Fort Pike, two recruits and three Indian scouts. Your Excellency, I suppose, could call out by courtesy the young gentlemen of your ' Governor's guard.' Are there fifty of them, all told? But while we keep up school drill, which I hope may be always, the Mayor of Tamworth may order out this pretty escort, as sure that they will appear as the Czar may be sure of the Imperial Guard."

And again, and fortunately, the little Clerk of Committees was satisfied, and permitted us to move. My own belief is that we had been waiting till a messenger from his wife told him that her party was all ready, in Seligman and Kroom's front windows. Then came the joyful " Forward, march," and we "proceeded," or "proceshed," as I observed the boys called our movement, to the open region where the Academy of Fine Art was to stand. It is in the northwestern part of the city, a part which has great natural advantages, I am told, but to which at that time the movement of population had not advanced. " Hold their lots too high," said Mr. Mole, who walked with me. But another gentleman afterwards assured me that the difficulty was that the lots had been held too low ; that the only way to sell real estate in such circumstances is to convince people that you have "the very best article." He said the purchasers did not know much about it themselves, and had not often an opinion ; that they wanted to go where other people went, and that you must hold it as you would hold a Meissonier picture, or a folio Shakespere at a round price and a high, when they would all rush for it as a trout jumps at a fly just above the water.

However this may be, there were then no houses in the neighborhood of the future Academy. The most pretentious building was a large platform, on which the Governor, the Mayor, the Aldermen, the Trustees and the invited guests, alas, were elevated above the level of the prairie, to join in the ceremonial and to be observed as they joined. I say "alas," because I was one of the three or four persons who were invited, having no official right to be present; and thus I was exposed with the others to the tenderness of a northwest wind, which was tearing its way across from the Northern Rockies, unbroken by any of those palaces which will curb such a wind more or less when the proper price shall have been found for the sale of those matchless sites for building.

I learned the next day how foolish I was, and what I should have done. Hardly had we begun on the "exercises" of the occasion—just at the moment, in fact, when Dr. Thursby said, "Let us pray," a sharp crack was heard, and, from my corner, I saw the Governor, the Lieutenant Governor, the military staff and others, who, but just before, had been a tall human line, shielding me a little from the Euroclydon of which I have spoken—I saw them, I say, all descending as they stood, without moving a muscle. It was just as one sees the clown descend at the theater. It spoke well for the courage of these men, that no one flinched, started or even turned pale. They went down as if this were a part of the ceremony, and as if they had been forewarned by the Clerk of Committees. Dr. Thursby was not so used to facing danger. He stopped in his prayer. The Mayor opened his eyes, and said, not very loudly, "Will every one stand still?" Then one by one he bade gentlemen jump off, till the Governor and others could do so safely. Then a hurried investigation was made by the President of the Mechanics' Association. That side of the platform had been badly built and had given way, "that was all," they said. The Governor privately told me afterwards that he wished that when they asked him again, they would put the Mayor and the Aldermen on the exposed sides. One or two shores of timber were hastily run under the platform, and the ceremony went on. Again Dr. Thursby began his prayer, and the printed programme, brief in this part, was followed through.

I say I learned by this experience where I should have been, and what I should have done. For I noticed the next day that this little incident, in which the lives of four or five men of prominence were in danger, was not so much as alluded to by the Argus-eyed and many-voiced press of Tamworth. I asked John Fisher if the managers had power enough to suppress the notice of a failure so mortifying. " Oh, no ! " he said, " you do not think those reporters were going out in that gale, do you? They had the printed programme, and knew the plan. They knew the wind was stiff and cold, and while we were laying the stone, they were all writing out their notes in the hall where we saw them afterwards. They did not know the thing happened. Nobody knows it, except you and I and two or three hundred people. And if you had known how to be comfortable, you would not have ' assisted.' "

" But you see I mean," said John, " that while you are at Tamworth you shall see all there is to be seen."

So, with very short ceremonial, the stone was laid. The silver trowel, which the ladies had provided, was presented in a short speech by their spokesman, who was a man, to the Chairman of the Committee of Arrangements. The chairman in another speech presented it to the Master of Ceremonies. In another speech he presented it to the President of the Board of Aldermen. He presented it to the Mayor in another, and he finally gave it to the Governor. The Governor was a prompt man, who had carried a musket at Fort Donelson, and had here learned the advantage of doing quickly, with few words, what you set out to do. He nodded to the chief Masonic character who was in attendance, and the stone was pronounced plumb and square, almost literally in what the native proverb calls " no time."

Then we were able to " proceed " again to the hall, where " the address," as the dialect of our time calls it, was to be made. People speak of " the address," on such an occasion : of " the oration," for instance, on the Fourth of July, as if it were always the same oration. They say Mr Stokes delivered "the oration," as if it had been kept in a cage since the last Fourth of July, and, on this anniversary, he let it out to run around a little while. So, on the laying of the corner-stone, we went to the Mechanics' Hall that we might hear " the address."

And here, for the first time, I found out where the singing was to be. I had learned that the ladies at our house were in a chorus somewhere, and I had supposed that we were to find them on the ground. But so soon as we stood in that northwester, I saw that that was a business for men only, and I asked Mr. Mole, my companion, vainly about the women. So soon as we came into the Mechanics' Hall, the mystery was solved. The Jubal Society was in full force, with a chorus of four hundred voices. A delegation even larger from the public schools occupied some of the largest balconies, and I was told that they were to sing also, and other societies.

All through this ceremonial, almost endless, I had been learning more and more where and how the enthusiasm had been roused, which made all the people of Tamworth give up their daily occupation and create (out of the whole cloth, I had been tempted to say) an Autumn Festival, in honor of this

"Academy of Fine Art," which was still to be. I understood better and better every hour that the Germans of the
town had set their hearts upon such an institution, and I
could see how prominent they were in the arrangements for
carrying it through. In the manufactories of every sort, it
happened almost always that Germans were the draftsmen.
And, as it happened, there went out from Tamworth a great
deal of work which needed artistic design and decoration.
Their enthusiasm in the Academy cause had been enough to
call out all the musical force, in which, as everywhere in the
world, they were such skilful leaders. This was the reason
why the Jubals and the Amphions, and, indeed, all the
musical societies of any note, were present at our festival.

I should not tell the history of it in such detail, but that I
was also learning, all along, more and more of the place
held by my friend Fisher in this community. I had noticed,
in the morning, that when the fussy little Master of Ceremonies was arranging us for our march, he was conscious that
John Fisher " belonged " somewhere, though he did not
know quite how to express it. He had a list of officials,
but John Fisher was not an official. From this list, he
called off Governor, Mayor, and all the dignitaries.
But, of a sudden, he looked at it with a certain despair,
and then, turning promptly to my friend, he said, " Mr.
Fisher comes here, with Governor Winterhalter ! " Governor Winterhalter being the most distinguished guest
present, the chief of the next State. Just so was it when
we were modestly arranging ourselves in the front of the
bass-drums on the great platform at the Mechanics' Hall.
We were all trying to obey the parable and to find the worst
seats, where all were pretty bad if one thought of enjoying the

music, when the little man, seeing a chair of honor immediately next our own Governor's, looked round wildly till he saw John Fisher, and said to him at once, "Mr. Fisher, you are to come here; you are to come here. This is your chair." As indeed it was. So soon as John Fisher came forward to it, modestly, the assembly recognized him and clapped loudly and long, showing indeed more real interest in him than they had shown in the more formal, courteous welcome they had given to the Governor.

No! It is fortunately not the business of this story to tell what the Chairman of the Committee of Arrangements said to that mass of six thousand people, nor what the Mayor said, nor what the Governor said, nor what the Chairman of the Building Committee said, nor the President of the Trustees, nor "the Orator of the day" when at the last he "delivered the oration" from the captivity of his portfolio. These words of wisdom, are they not written in the *Tamworth Chronicle* and the *Tamworth Record* of that evening and the next morning? Nay, were not enterprising newsboys selling them under the windows before the overture by Wagner was finished, so that, in a sense, that captive oration was delivered before Dr. Witherspoon untied the ribbons of his portfolio?

We were only four hours and a half in the hall. After the overture, we began on what the ungodly would call a variety entertainment, sandwiching our music and addresses quite evenly. Between two speeches would come a "Hymn written for the occasion," or an "Ode written for the occasion," or the song of praise, or a triumphal chorus. After the oration was delivered, and the manuscript was again confined within its limits, we sang "America" with such zeal that it was a wonder the roof did not rise. Then a benediction was pronounced by Dr. Thursby, and then— "Then," says the reader, a little tired, having, indeed, been turning the page to see what would come next, "then it was all done!"

Dear reader, this shows how little you know about such things. I am sure you skip when you read the newspapers. The celebration was by no means ended. The real celebration was just now to begin. The speeches we had been making were our offering on the throne of dignity and decorum. Now we were to celebrate as we wanted to.

Fortunately for all concerned, the raging storm of the morning had blown itself out. By some divine change of a center, or other formality known to the Signal Sergeants, the wind had come into the southwest, and was breathing on us from the Indian's heaven. For the last hour of that delicious autumn day, we stood again on our platform of the morning, which had been thoroughly repaired by a corps of carpenters while we had been singing and speaking and listening. And now there passed by jolly companies of tradesmen, each with the devices of their craft, to lay flowers on the stone; companies of scholars, companies of singers, all sorts of companies. All this had been planned and executed, one could see in a minute, by German ingenuity. I felt as if I were in Antwerp, by the side of my grandmother's great-great-grandfather, after some splendid victory. Children prettily dressed in fancy costumes, jolly blacksmiths, singing as they marched, trained companies representing this or that triumph of the Arts, passed by in rapid succession. And from each, without the "march past" being stopped, would run forward a pretty girl, or a fine boy,

or a young woman, or a more awkward man, with a wreath
or a cross, or a basket of flowers, to place it on the corner-
stone, and to say, " I pledge the interest of the Girls'
Friendly Union," or " The men of Kroom's Hollow will
not be forgotten," or " The children promise the fathers to
maintain what they begin," or in some other fashion to express an interest in that to which the day was dedicat-
ed. Beautiful teams of horses, in one case eight exquisite
white oxen, dragged along great platforms on which were
pretty tableaux repeating some of the great pictures of the
world. I have never lost the memory of a Diana, so well-
dressed, playing so prettily with a pet fawn, and yet with
an air so thoroughly antique and Grecian that I never see
the cast of the Diana of the Louvre without recalling that
pretty figure.

And, as every one of these companies passed, its enthusiastic Marshal, after he had called for " three cheers for the
new Academy," would call again for " three more for John
Fisher." He would do this certainly, whether he remembered the Governor, or forgot him. And the cheers for my modest friend, John Fisher, always came " with a will."

I had hoped that I might have the pleasure of going
home with Miss Bell. But, when the fête was over, she was
nowhere to be seen. Fisher seemed to know where to find
the other ladies, and without delay we took up Mrs. Fisher
and Mrs. Grattan, and the rest of the party. As it happened,
Mrs. Grattan and I rode home together, and I asked her about
this regular tribute to John Fisher. " Had he many
Germans in his employ?" I said.

"Oh, no! it is not that," she said. "It is—well, simply it is that he deserves it, Germans? No! You are

right in thinking that these clubs and societies have been marshaled so prettily by Germans. But I do not think there are many Germans in his mills. No. It is not that. It is —well, Mr. Mellen, it is that he helps all these things along. He lends a hand, as you Wadsworth people say. If a cricket club wants to put up a pavilion, he subscribes. If the Wagner people want some new instruments, they go to him. He takes an interest; that is what it means. They know they have one friend, who has risen from the ranks, and who has not forgotten them."

CHAPTER XIV.

"WHERE in the world is Mary Bell?" So did Mrs. Fisher question us, as we sat down to our well-earned, late dinner. "As for my husband I never expect him; and Mary Bell is as little to be relied on as he is; off there—it is lucky, Mr. Mellen, that there is one person, not above vulgar bread and butter, in this house."

The truth was, so far as I had seen it since I was her guest, that Miss Bell had been present at every meal, at the moment the company assembled. So had Mr. Fisher until to-day. This evening he was dining with the Trustees of the Academy. Mrs. Fisher herself had had fully half her meals in her own room.

But this was only her piquant way of speaking.

We had scarcely begun our dinner, however, when a servant came in and called me out. "A young woman is very eager to see you, and says she cannot wait."

Sure enough, I found in the hall a woman, I might well

say a girl, with her face pale and marked with tears. I led her into a room on one side, made her sit down, almost unwillingly, and said, " What is the matter? Why do you want to see me?"

She found it very hard to answer. She sobbed before she did answer. " I am so sorry. You will think I am crazy. But, indeed—I know I ought to come—I wanted, you know. No, you do not know—I asked for Mr. Fisher, and he is not in. But I could not come to-morrow—you are his friend?"

I suppose I looked uneasy, as these incoherencies ran on. In truth, I thought she was crazy.

She laughed, in a wild way. " You think I am crazy. No, no. I will tell you." Then in a perfectly distinct and business-like way she said, " Tell Mr. Fisher that he must not go to the ratification meeting Thursday. The plan is all made that he shall be put to shame to his face. I am so sorry, but my husband is in the plan. And Mr. William Salter is to make a speech, and tell all about the necklace !"

I was now sure she was crazy. But I said, " Necklace ! What necklace?"

" Do you tell Mr. Fisher what I tell you to tell him, that William Salter will tell the people all about the necklace. Mr. Fisher will know."

And with that she was gone.

CHAPTER XV.

A S the election drew nearer and nearer, I found myself more and more interested in it, although as a stranger I could not interfere much with the various plans which were discussed around me, and would not indeed, if I could. My time never hung heavy. Thanks to my friend the Boss, and to public spirit like his, which I found was a general matter in Tamworth, it was a place where a stranger could live for three weeks, and yet not end those weeks by suicide. The people were hard at work, but were social. After I became acquainted among them I found I could make a visit without exciting the suspicion of the servant-girl who took my card to her mistress. She did not seem to think I came for the parlor clock or the spoons, as they do seem to think in most of the cities to which my vagrant life tempts me. They do not run to club houses in Tamworth, as in some other places I know. Clubs there are, unnumbered and innumerable. But what with galleries, reading-rooms, libraries, museums, " exchanges of literature," " exchanges of art," and the rest, there are a plenty of " loafing places," if one may use the vernacular. Now a " loafing place " is what a stranger most needs.

There was a good-natured fellow named Sturgeon (if I might use the vernacular again so soon, I should say he was Yankee " clever"), who had opened a house of accommodation, which had many imitations. But his was the original " Saint's Rest." That was its name in gold letters over the door. I need hardly say that John Fisher had furnished him the funds for a beginning, but the success of the enterprise had long ago made Sturgeon independent, and he had repaid John. The " Saint's Rest " was just off the Main street, on one of those narrow cross streets which trade avoids, but still central. Any one might go there. So you may to an ordinary hotel, but you are not wanted at a regular hotel, unless you come for a meal. Here, they would give you a cup of coffee or a slice of toast, but that was not what they were for. They were there, and the "Saint's Rest" was open, that you might have a "loafing place."

If you had an appointment with a man at eleven, and the clock obstinately announced ten-thirty, you went to the "Saint's Rest," paid ten cents as you entered, and then were free of the lower stories of the house—indeed, of almost all of it. There was a great newspaper room ; there was a great room full of novels and magazines. They took seventy-nine copies of the first number of *Lend a Hand*. There were writing-desks, with paper, pens and ink. There were directories and cyclopædias and telegraph blanks. There were long, deep sofas, if a man wanted his nap. There were smoking-rooms. It was in fact a club, where you chose yourself and expelled yourself, and in which there was no assessment after you paid the initiation fee. This fee, as I said, was ten cents. You paid it at the door, and went in. At the end of an hour, a boy found you and asked you for another ten cents, if you wanted to stay another hour. Practically you never did want to. No one ever wants to stay in such a place more than an hour. But he may want very much to stay in such a place fifteen minutes, when there is no such place at hand.

Sturgeon established the "Saint's Rest" with such success, that six or eight other Sturgeons of different names followed his example. He did a very good business, enlarged his house by adding all the neighboring houses—never rebuilt it—so that it had all the coziness of home house-building, and often, as he told me, he received a thousand people a day there. Now that I recur to it, I suppose the convenience of such places may have been the reason why there were so few other club-houses in Tamworth.

If you think of it, a " club-house " is a hotel kept by a committee of gentlemen who were never trained to the business of hotel-keeping. And its first rules are directed to the question how it can keep out the people who would like to come in.

For John Fisher himself, his comfortable and pretty office at the works was his club-house, and there you might often meet agreeable people not too busy. He left us, as had been said, soon after breakfast every day, and we were then left to our own devices. Not long after the laying of the corner-stone, I found one day that there was no drive in prospect, or other morning plan which gave me an excuse for waiting on Miss Bell's movements or Mrs. Grattan's, and I accordingly started alone to walk down town. I had hardly passed into the street, from the avenue, when Miss Bell overtook me, in the carriage which she always used, and she bade the coachman stop and ask me if she might not take me down.

"Or are you walking for pleasure?" she asked, laughing, as I took my seat gladly, and shut the door.

I told her that I should be glad to take my exercise at some other time. If I had dared I should have said something which would have been absolutely true, as to the pleasure she gave me. But, with this woman, one avoided by instinct all the conventional pretences, and I was therefore, in this case, afraid to tell the truth. I did say that to give the traveler " a lift " seemed to be a work of mercy, which in modern life belongs with feeding the hungry and giving clothes to the naked.

"Which is, as it happens, just what I am starting upon," she said; "and unless you are in a hurry, I shall make you stop at the Diet Kitchen. If you are in a hurry, you must do as the canal-boat people do."

"I must go afoot?" said I.

"Yes. But I will not keep you long." Then she told, briefly, of the suffering in ·a family which the Charity Organization of Tamworth entrusted to her. "I am afraid the battle is fought, though," she said. "All we can do now is to bind up the wounds and retreat with honor."

I was glad enough to see the Diet Kitchen, a perfectly neat and well-organized bureau, occupying the ground floor of a house on a cross street. The attendants were all ladies, many of whom I had met at John Fisher's music parties, whist parties, or dinner parties. This was the day of weekly service, chosen by these particular people, and I think no single detail of this ministry for the sick was left by them to any hired hands. The gift was Love from the beginning to the end.

Miss Bell took what she wanted for her patient, giving me the chance to carry to the carriage this basket and that can, gave the coachman her direction, and we started again. But this time we were to stop at a fruit shop. Just at that season those Western cities make a display of pomp, crimson, scarlet, topaz, and gold—of color and glory which cannot be named, such as the gorgeous East with lavish hand cannot surpass, if indeed it can rival. Let the sated traveler, who is tired of picture galleries and has "done" every catalogued museum in the world, stay over a train some day in October that he may see the marvels of the fruit shops of Rochester. Two or three more baskets, of late peaches, of

early pears, and of grapes in season, were put into the carriage and then she said "Birnebaum's," and the carriage
dived into the canal region of the town. Clearly the coachman knew where he was going.

"And here I must leave you, Mr. Mellen," said my
companion. "Hiram will take you where you wish to go,
and come back for me."

But I begged that I might carry the baskets in. Perhaps
I might be of use.

"No one is of use," she said sadly. "As for poor
Birnebaum, he is too weak to see any one whose face he
does not know. But you can, of course, bring in the
baskets. Stay with your horses, Hiram. Mr. Mellen will
come with me."

And we went in and up the stairs. A two-story house, where
the poor people we sought occupied the upper floor. I went
with one set of baskets, returned to the carriage for the fruit,
and waited at the head of the stairs some minutes for any
one to guide me further.

Miss Bell then appeared in tears. "I am sorry to make
you wait," she said. "But it is at the very end. He will
not live an hour. I did not suppose all was so nearly over.
And his poor wife—and his mother——"

She sat on the window-seat, in the narrow entry way.
silent for a moment, and I saw that she was a little puzzled.
Once more I said, "Can I do anything, go anywhere?"

"Thank you," she said in a half unconscious way, and
then roused herself. "Yes, if you will. I was going to ask
John to send me a messenger boy. But—but—if you will,
Mr. Mellen——" and without finishing her sentence she
wrote on a leaf of her diary, tore out the page, and folded it

in an envelope which she carried with her. She addressed this in pencil and gave it to me.

I did not look at the letter, but asked her where I should take it.

" He is at the Iroquois Building, the number is 73, you will find it on the note. I would send Hiram but he must drop you at the Avenue. He goes home for Cordelia Grattan. You might say at lunch that we may be here all day. There is everything to do." And then, with the absent-mindedness of a person wholly engrossed in one affair, she left me almost abruptly, without saying good-by, and went back into the sick room.

I knew where the Iroquois Block was, perfectly well. It was a great columbarium of lawyers' and architects' and doctors' offices. I took it for granted that the note she gave me was to some doctor who had been in attendance. I was not likely to forget any word she had spoken to me. I hurried to the place, which was, perhaps, a mile away. I took the elevator up, and bade the boy drop me at 73.

" Third door on the right," said the boy, after we paused on our flight toward heaven.

I came to the door to read on the sign, " George Rossiter."

CHAPTER XVI.

LUNCH proved to be an early dinner. And early dinner proved to be a dinner party. We did not have Cordelia Grattan or Miss Bell, as she had warned us. But we did have a large party of what I must call the literary people of

Tamworth, including quite a scattering from the college and
the "seminary," and several of the newspaper men.   For
ladies, we had Mrs. Stetson, who edited the children's de-
partment of the organ of the Reformed Covenanters ; Miss
Porter, who was the head of a successful girls' school at
Ponceau, the other side of the river ; a Miss Flinders, whom
no one explained to me, and a German lady who was called
the Countess, as I observed, when we spoke behind her
back, but whom one addressed as Madame Anstell.   We
were fourteen without our own two ladies, for whom excuses
were made.   I soon saw that I and the Countess, Dr. Knapp,
and Mr. Keane, were all comparative strangers, and that there
was the necessary friction before the party could warm up.
We had the inevitable talk as to English pronunciation and
American, whether one says " either " or " either," " trait "
or " tray," with the old stories about " nice " and " nasty,"
but after one or two courses, having felt each other's force
and parry, we were more at ease and talk became free.
Mrs. Fisher, when there was the slightest risk of a rut,
would upset the whole carriage by one of her rudenesses or
follies, and this gave us no bad chance to begin again.

In her light and festive way she told us that she was de-
serted by her two ladies, and if this was a party of men
with no women who could cheer it up it was no fault of hers.
This was agreeable to the four ladies who were her guests.
Then she cheered up those who sat around her by an account
of the sufferings of the Birnebaum family, and an account,
drawn from imagination, of Mr. Birnebaum's death.   Then
she said that for her part she wished she were with
the widow, that she took no pleasure but in ministering to
such grief, and that she could not understand how any woman

could stay away from such calls.   At the same time she seemed able to join in conversation with the gentleman and lady at her right and left, and to trifle with the provision which Mrs. Edwards had made for us.   She afterwards, on another view of the subject, said that Cordelia Grattan and Mary Bell were both impulsive creatures, governed merely by passing fancies ; that their absence in the distressed household was merely a whim of the moment, and that any hired nurse would have done all that they did, vastly better.

Mr. Emerson charges us to read no book till it has been published a year.   He says that so many books are wholly forgotten before the year is over that one thus saves a great deal of time.   I am not brave enough to obey him.   And I thought myself well up in the current literature.   But these people silenced and confounded me.   They looked with scorn on any one who had not digested the last *Fortnightly*, the last *Revue* and the last biography, it being at that moment the life of the Hessian general Rahl, by his great grandson's brother-in-law.   I was reminded by their facility of the well-known readiness of the bright Boston circles.   The first day a stranger meets them, he wonders at their omniscience.   Every one knows the Himalayan passes.   Every one discusses Sanskrit and Prakrit.   Every one is at home in the Fiji islands.   At his next dinner party every one discusses Virgil's meters, and Mad. de Staël's grandfather, and the laws of enharmonics.   And he still marvels at the wonders of culture.   Before the third meeting, however, he has found out that they all read *Littell's Living Age* ; he also subscribes and then is as bright as the rest of them.   What interested me in the Tamworth people was that they were

so perfectly up to time, and so indifferent about questions
which had been on the carpet a year ago.   As the Mackinaw
editor said to Dr. Farrar, "Dante is played out."

But we had too many editors and too many people of con-
science not to drift round to the very latest subject and most
engrossing, which was for them, as for the rest of the world,
the coming election.   I was very much interested to see
that these people of books, even the editors among them,
were affected by the political crisis, in a way quite different
from that in which it had aroused the business representa-
tives of the wards, or from that in which my Temperance
friends looked at it.   The fact that in the neighboring city
of Putnam, "THEY," (always "They,") had put a man in,
as keeper of the public library, who did not know a line of
French from a line of Italian, exasperated these people
twenty times as much as would the fact that, in the same
city of Putnam, " they " had made the repairs of the jail
cost forty-seven thousand dollars, when thirty thousand
would have built a new jail.   And when I intimated to my
next neighbor, a distinguished man of letters there, that the
reason why they needed any jail in Putnam, which was not
a county town, was that they chose to do all the liquor
retailing for the rest of the county, I saw at once that he
counted me as simply a fanatic from that moment, and that
there was no great use in talking to me, except for civility.
But it mattered very little whether he talked to me or not,
for the conversation became general, and we all rushed pell-
mell into the details of the canvass, quite as eagerly as had
the evening party I have before described, though not with
as much system.   If there ever were an etiquette which de-
layed talk on politics till the ladies left the table, that eti-

quette was violated now. No one was more eager than they were, nor any one more amusing than Mrs. Fisher.

"I tell my husband that, if he would only let us vote, we would settle all this at the first election. To begin with, we would not have any of this nonsense about aldermen and common council. I wish I knew the difference. I believe there is none. I am quite sure Mr. Beltridge, the super-intendent of our Sunday-school, told me he was a council-man, and then when I wanted him to pardon Jane Flaherty's husband out of jail, not six months after, Mr. Fisher told me he was an alderman, and had nothing to do with it. No, Mr. Keane, I should have the same number of aldermen as of councilmen, and then they could not be opposing each other as they do. If there were no mayor at all we should get on a great deal better. But I tell Mr. Fisher that no woman, who knows a woman's place, can think for a moment of voting, etc., etc., etc.," poor Mr. Keane being the only person who could rightly repeat this part of my story.

"But the news of the day," said Mr. Visdon, the editor-in-chief of the *Chronicle*, "is that Michael Swinton has been appointed one of the Commissioners to the International Fair at Antwerp. His commission came from Washington this morning. He means to accept, and so the question as to the Seventh Ward must be fought all over again."

Let us hope that a patient reader remembers that Michael Swinton led the Street in its conflict with the Hill in that region.

"Then Col. Stothers will walk over," said I, hoping to show my intelligence, and really, as usually happens when one shows off his intelligence, showing that I was a fool. The editor did not so much as look at me, nor form any sort of reply. Such a question deserved no answer. But Professor Greene said, with a frightened tenderness for me, "Oh dear, no! Col. Stothers would no more unite—unite—our friends there, than would—than would—well, any one you could name."

We had all looked at John Fisher when this new problem was brought up. The question of Alderman in Ward Seven had become much more interesting—it probably was more important—than the question of the vote for Mayor, where, indeed, we felt quite sure. But, if we lost the Seventh Ward, the whole fabric of our system would give way.

I do not know if Mr. Visdon thought that his news would surprise John Fisher. Perhaps he did. For it was certain that Michael Swinton had told him, in secrecy, that he received the appointment, just an hour before, without even applying for it, or thinking of it, and that at that time no other man in Tamworth knew it. It was also certain that Fisher had just come from the mills and had met Visdon on the door-steps. So it is possible Visdon thought that he had, for once, a bit of local news which even John Fisher did not have.

But, if Mr. Visdon had known what Mr. Fisher told me that evening, that so soon as the difficulty in Ward Seven took place he had himself written to the Secretary of State, at Washington, to ask that this place or something like it might be given to Michael Swinton, which would take him out of the canvass; if Mr. Visdon had known that three or four private letters had passed from each side, and that, the morning before, Mr. Fisher had a long despatch in cipher from Washington, I think he would not have supposed that this anecdote took John Fisher by surprise.

"I knew I had some influence in Washington," said John to me afterwards. - "Of course I would not use it for myself, but for the public I would. What am I for? If Michael Swinton spends next year in Antwerp he will be much more fit to be an alderman when he comes home."

At the table, however, the talk ran fast and loud as to what could be done in the ward. Col. Stothers would never withdraw. He had pledged too much and had gone too deep. The Hill people were on a "regular bender." It was their first experiment in politics in many years, and they rather liked it. And yet there was as little chance of their choosing Col. Stothers as there was of their choosing the lead statue of Meriwether Lewis, which stood in their pretty little park.

"Such a shame that we should lose Ward Seven," said Miss Flinders to me.

John Fisher had said almost nothing. It seemed to me that he had been, almost with affectation, discussing Lohengrin with the Countess, who was on his right. Miss Flinders and I were well down the table on his left. It was, therefore, the more marked, when he, as if he heard every word which everybody said at his own table, took up Miss Flinders at once and said:

"Do not be distressed, Miss Flinders. We shall not lose Ward Seven. We shall carry it by the strongest vote we have had for years. All your funny quarrel there has done no end of good. Your kid-gloved friends have taught us how to carry on a canvass."

"I am glad they have taught anybody anything," said Miss Flinders, who had the courage of her convictions, was, as it happened, the only person present who lived in the ward, was a child of the public, a perfect lady, and defied the Hill people and all their elegant buckram and precision. "But I should be glad to be let into the secret, and know how this is to be done. For one, I want to vote. I do not agree with Mrs. Fisher."

For Mrs. Fisher's third and last oracle on this subject had been that no woman should ever wish to vote, and that no decent woman ever said she did. She had three times expressed herself on the other side of the same subject since dinner began.

"You do not suppose that Col. Stothers wants to stand, do you?" asked John Fisher, quizzically.

"I know he is no coward," said she, doubting to what this must lead, and knowing that she must commit herself to nothing, in a conflict of wits with him.

"No one ever thought him a coward," said John seriously. "You canal people may laugh at him as you choose, he is a gentleman born and bred. He loves his country and would die for it, as readily as on the day when he was the first man on the breastworks at Fort Donelson. He would withdraw this moment, if he were here, and if we showed him a better man."

"A better man? Yes," said Keane, "but the trouble is to persuade him and the Hill that we have found a better man."

"It would be hard to name a better man, in the true sense," said John Fisher. "A better man than Col. Stothers is does not walk this earth, if by goodness you mean honor, truth, generosity, pluck; yes, and modesty. But he will not be trampled on, more than Michael Swinton. All you have to do is to show him a candidate who on the whole knows this city, its schools, its poorhouse, its roads, its people, better than he does."

" And that is hard to find," said Keane again, Keane being the leader of a coterie, not unlike the Hill coterie, in Ward
One, where they had things all their own way. "Hard, I
mean, in Ward Seven."

Miss Flinders's eyes were flashing fire. She was about to
give " that little Keane" an answer which would have en-
venomed the politics of the town for years, when John Fisher, who was not going to give her a chance, said :

"I will give you your man. And Col. Stothers will withdraw in his favor, and all the Stothers horses will work all
day carrying voters to the polls for him. And Miss Maud
Flinders will wave her handkerchief when the new alderman
is cheered in the evening by the people in the Hollow."

"You are a wizard, Mr. Fisher," she said, but you must
wave your wand before I believe. Who is your candidate?"

" Col. Stothers's next door neighbor !"

Miss Flinders dropped the orange she was peeling.

" Dr. Witherspoon ! Dr. Witherspoon an alderman ! "

"Precisely," said Mr. Fisher. "Dr. Witherspoon an
alderman. Dr. Witherspoon knows as much of drainage as
he knows of Greek, and that is to say he knows the matter
to the bottom ; he knows men by instinct, he knows the
schools of Tamworth as no supervisor of them all does, he is
a man of that simplicity and that honor that no man dares
speak of fraud within a mile of him. He is liberal to every
form of opinion, and he has the courage of his convictions.
Now what are we to have aldermen for, as Mrs. Fisher says,
if we may not choose such a man as that when we need him,
or Col. Stothers when we need him?"

Thus was it, I think, that Dr. Witherspoon was first nominated. What is more, I believe he was flattered as well as surprised when he heard of the nomination.

To me, as we sat together that evening, after the rest of the party had gone away, Fisher opened himself rather more confidentially on the subject of local politics than ever before.

I rallied him a little on the nomination of Dr. Witherspoon. "Ah, well," he said, "as well to nominate him at a dinner party as a caucus. One must move somewhere. I wanted Miss Flinders, who is a power 'in the street,' to have the comfort of thinking that she was a prominent agent in his election, as she will be. She is a pillar in his church, and a loyal public-spirited woman." Then he told me what I have revealed to the reader, that he and the Secretary of State together, had thought our honest and stubborn friend, Michael Swinton, would do good service at Antwerp, and that it was thus that a vacancy was created in the ticket for aldermen, which must be instantly filled.

"It has all turned out very well," he said. "When the canvass began those people would no more have let us have their 'dear Dr. Witherspoon' on the Board, than they would have burned his church down while he was preaching. But now the Greeks were at their doors, literally. They had carried their ridiculous Swinton-Stothers quarrel so far that they were within a week of choosing the master of a grog-shop to the Board, and three common councilmen of his own kidney. They will begin to learn that no man is too good for this sort of service."

I asked if he did not find himself annoyed and provoked in the midst of such conflicts.

"Sometimes annoyed, never provoked, often amused," said he. And then it was that he opened his confidence to me a little. "I have large interests in this town," he said. "Pride apart, I have a large pecuniary interest in having it well governed. It is now six years since I saw that decent people were deserting the business of governing it. That business was running into the hands of adventurers, bartenders, horse-jockeys, gamblers, what you call ring-men. Why, I tried to choose a decent school committee. I found I was considered as interfering with the prerogatives of a set of drunken hounds whom I would not speak to in a street-car.

"Well, I set to considering this thing. I said to myself, 'Suppose I had a fancy for yachting. Or suppose I wanted to buy folio Shaksperes and original Miltons. Or suppose I had taken to Corots, and Calames, and Meissoniers, like your Mrs. Morgan or Mr. Vanderbilt. How much should I gladly spend a year in that business? Why, I should readily spend a hundred thousand dollars the first year for my yacht, and fifty thousand a year afterwards.' I laid aside those amounts in my plans for the next six years. Of course I never bought a man or a vote. But I put the money where I thought it would help in the good government of the city. I put it in reading-rooms, and boys' institutes, and music-clubs, and libraries, and Sunday-schools, and galleries, and turner matches, and gymnasiums, and law-and-order leagues, and a thousand other agencies which enthusiasts are constantly inventing. The consequence is that I am the friend of the enthusiasts and they are friends of mine.

"And, Mellen, it is always the enthusiasts who win in the long run, if they have a man of sense behind them. Nothing ever succeeded in this' world, which had not a crazy man hitched on somewhere.

"That was the first consequence, I say. The second, if you ever choose to go into the same line of business, was this. When I began, my taxes in this city were sixteen on the thousand, I paid sixteen dollars on every thousand of my assessment. Now I pay eight on the thousand, just half what it was, and the government is much better than it used to be. They assess me for about two millions. So I save in my own taxes rather more than a hundred and fifty thousand dollars a year. Practically it costs me nothing to run my yacht, and I enjoy the fun of sailing her."

CHAPTER XVII.

I SHOULD have said that I knew what John Fisher's life was, in all its important details, after I had been in Tamworth for a fortnight of such experiences as I have described. But one of those coincidences turned up, which are frequent enough in daily life and on the stage, but which writers who are not dramatists are always afraid of, which show in truth how small the world is, and it gave me quite a new glimpse of the way in which part of his time was taken.

There had been another state dinner party at his house. For a set of French gentlemen had turned up, commissioned by their government to inquire into the condition of prisons or of something, and they had letters of introduction to John Fisher, and so we had them to dinner. We were full forward in the ceremony, but I was doing my best with the particular pundit who was entrusted to me on one side, and a frightened school girl on the other, who had been asked because the pundits had been hospitably received by her father in Duluth. Of a sudden, one of the servants spoke to me and gave me a letter, which he said came by the latest delivery and was marked, rather boldly, "IMMEDIATE."

I was afraid of bad news from a friend who was ill, and, as soon as I well could, opened my letter to find that I need not have been so anxious. But Carmichael, who was an old friend of mine, and was now settled down in Edenton, in North Carolina, had fallen in with a newspaper giving an account of our terrible railroad accident, at the Lookout Station, the day of the wash-out. In the account was the name of Mrs. Winborn among the killed, and the name of a certain Nathan Winborn, as badly wounded. "Now I see by the same paper that you are to come to this same Tamworth," so Carmichael went on; "and I beg you to find if this Mr Winborn is my old Captain in the 11th Kentucky. He is the noblest fellow I ever knew, if he is, and you must bear him my best love, and see if you can do anything for him. There is no man living, whom I love and honor as I do him."

Of course, there was no reason why I should feel that this commission of Carmichael's must be attended to immediately. But I tell all this story about the dinner simply to explain why I went in search of Col. Winborn when I did, and how the coincidence took place to which I referred. For, after dinner, when other guests came in, rather tired, to say the truth, of the prisons, and of talking bad French, I thought I would see if the poor man were anywhere in our part of the town, and so slipped out, unobserved, into the splendid moonlight. It would not take long to ride into the city on a street-car, and there I could determine whether I would or would not go in search of my man. Naturally, I should have asked advice of the home party. But they were all engaged with their guests, and I was glad to paddle my own canoe.

But I had the inevitable drawbacks. The directory revealed " Nathan Winborn, 53 Laurel," very plainly. Certainly, there could not be in the world many people of that name. But I saw, with a certain regret, that the directory revealed nothing more. Now when a man's name is in the directory, without any other token than that he lives somewhere, you know that he is either very high on the ladder of comfort or very low. He is so grand that he has no occupation but to fret over his investments, in which case that occupation is not put down, for reasons not known to me. Or he is so unfortunate that no one will employ him. And then you feel afraid that the wolf is at the door. In Nathan Winborn's case the " Laurel Street" was not encouraging. I had never heard of Laurel Street, nor had the somewhat cynical, though courteous druggist's clerk, whose chained directory I was consulting. I asked him, timidly, if he knew where Laurel Street was, and his reply showed that no man, well-to-do in the world, knew or cared. This was clear from the tone in which he said, " No, Sir!" No Laurel streets for such as him.

But the friendly directory revealed again that Laurel Street ran from 173 Garfield Street across to 99 Hancock Street. And these streets were in a distant suburb of the city. I doubted whether I should find Nathan Winborn that evening. The courteous clerk told me what line of street-cars I was to take, and that I should find them at the

City Hall. At the City Hall it proved that the car went to Hancock Street every half hour when the Omaha train was not late, as that night it probably was. All this ended by my walking a mile, taking the car when it passed me, and then, when I modestly asked to be dropped at Laurel Street, I was told with surprise, and scorn even, that I should have transferred at Baldwin's, that I had been switched off and was now on Grover Street, which was far away from Garfield Street, in short, that the best thing for me, was to leave the car at once and walk back again, all which I did accordingly. The reader will not wonder, then, that it was nearly ten o'clock before I found Nathan Winborn's house. I had determined not to ring, or make any sign, unless there seemed to be lights below stairs.

Alas, when I found the house, No. 53, my presages, gradually growing more doleful and more, acquired a sad certainty. This particular Garfield, and Arthur, and Laurel suburb was, clearly enough, no abode of splendor. The people were not at the top of the comfort ladder. No. 53 was a little " five-room house." Even in the moonlight I could see that it had but little paint, and it might have been, probably had been, moved from site to site half-a-dozen times, since some pioneer erected it, as various streets became more and more grand, and its place in them had been taken by more substantial homes. In all the rest of the street, the houses were as dark as at midnight. Either nobody else lived in Laurel Street, or they were all early people, who would not waste their kerosene. But Nathan Winborn's house showed a light from every window. It must be fully occupied with people who were awake.

After a moment's hesitation, therefore, I turned the little

crank in the middle of the door, and struck the little gong
on the other side within. I had to wait a full minute for an
answer. Then to my surprise, as the door was flung open,
the man who held a lamp above his head that he might see
his late visitor was John Fisher ! He was in his shirt-
sleeves.

"Is it you ?" he said, quick, anxious, and in a low tone.
"Nothing wrong at home, I hope." And in a moment I
re-assured him ; told him, indeed, that I had left home
while he was still in his own parlor, and that I had been
two hours in coming. "No," I said, "I found my way by
the directory to inquire about this poor gentleman. Was
he an officer in a Kentucky regiment in the war?"

"The same," said he, in the low voice in which he had
spoken before. "Poor fellow, he is at this moment dying
in his room. The doctor is with him, and says it cannot
last long. But I have sent the children to bed ; those are
their rooms up-stairs and the day-nurse is sleeping here."
He pointed to the rear room, which opened from the little
passage where we stood. "I cannot ask you in, you see,
unless, indeed, we should explore the kitchen. If, as I
suppose, you came to be of use to him, I am afraid there is
nothing more we can ask you to do. He will be with his
wife and baby before morning. The baby, you know, was
crushed with her mother."

I told him that I knew nothing, but that I came to be of
use, and, if it were of any use, I could easily spend the night
there.

"No," said John Fisher, perfectly simply, "he knows
me ; he is used to me. We will not make any change to-
night. This is my night, you see. But do not let us stand

talking here; they will wonder where you are, at home; and I will show you a shorter way than you came by. Really, really, I am all the force that they need. You see the doctor is here, and will be here till midnight. Stay, I will tell him I am going with you, and we can talk as we walk, in the open air.

He went in, for a moment, to the dying man's room; came back, and said he was sleeping gently, and then joined me to show me the direct way home. " I knew nothing of them," he said when we were well out of the house, "till the evening of the accident. One of our fellows, Hastings, went to the station when the doctor's train came in, and brought poor Winborn to his house. For Winborn begged to come home. It would have been better, perhaps, to have taken him to the hospital; but here were the children, three not hurt besides the two that were; and the poor fellow has been so much happier to have them where he could see them at any moment. So I am glad that Hastings brought him here. We had, of course, all the force which you could handle in that little cabin, and the doctors have been untiring. It is Lincoln who is with him now."

I told Mr. Fisher who Carmichael was, and repeated, as well as I could, the words of his eager letter. He had said that Nathan Winborn was a fellow-officer and one of the noblest men who ever lived. He had written to me to be sure that he might know what had befallen his friend. Then I asked, imprudently perhaps, "You speak of Hastings. Do I know him? Who is he? Who are 'we'?"

" Oh!" he replied, with an instant's hesitation, "there is a little knot of us; there are ten in all, who have kept together since we were all at the bench, and have sometimes counted in a new member to fill up a gap. We have found it a good thing to take the care—well, of such a thing as this, when it comes along, for ourselves and by ourselves, without making any fuss about it. And it is a good thing. I am very glad to be counted in still. Some things cannot be done by proxy; and I think it is always bad for a man to be separated, by whatever circumstances, from the rank and file, from all sorts and conditions of men. I wish I had known this fine Major Winborn before. I could have been of use to him, and he to me. But, as I have not known him, I am glad to take care of him here in person now; glad not to relegate everybody and everything to somebody else to see to. I was glad to split the wood for his kitchen fire, and to draw the tea which he wanted, after his own army fashion.

"The truth is, Mellen, that we ought never to lose the touch of the elbow, even if it happen, as things come and go, that you are serving on the staff. Do you remember—no; you were not with us—that fine fellow, Denny, when we were all drilling, just before Sumpter? I have never forgotten one of his saws: 'A man never knows his manual too well.' There is a deal in it. Those boys of mine should never ride a horse, if they could not saddle him, bridle him, and groom him. I believe I ought to say shoe him. And I swear to you, Mellen, I should feel cheap enough, if I were ever laid up with a broken leg, with a lot of women bothering about me to take care of me, if I had not found some chance to take my turn. That is the reason why I am on duty to-night. It does not happen often. But I should be very loath not to take my turn with the others. I cling to this Ten, of the old days, as I do not to any of the grander clubs. When it is my turn, as it is to-night, I am glad the night comes round."

And he bade me good-night, and went back to close poor Winborn's eyes.

CHAPTER XVIII.

WHEN the day of the ratification meeting came, I had, of course, determined to go. To my surprise, Mrs. Grattan and Miss Bell insisted on going also, and claimed my escort, which I was very willing to give. The woman whom I thought crazy had bidden me tell Mr. Fisher that William Salter would tell the people all about the necklace. I had thought she might be crazy, but still I did not dare neglect her message. I had fallen into the habit of asking Miss Bell's advice and information, when Tamworth life puzzled me. But I did not dare do that now, for the communication was clearly confidential.

So I simply told John Fisher, after waiting, in rather a cowardly way, for a day or two, that a woman had called me out to say that he must not go to the ratification meeting, for that William Salter would make a speech and tell the people all about the necklace.

I could not doubt for an instant but he was annoyed. There passed over his face a shadow, which I never saw but two or three times. And I never wanted to see it again. It expressed utter bitterness, with the sense of failure, and perhaps a sort of tired look, as if one should say: "What is the use of fighting any longer?" But it was gone in the infinitesimal of a second, and he might well fancy that I had never seen it. He lifted his great eyebrows as if in surprise, and said: "What in the world did she mean?" But he said nothing more. And I knew that he knew what she meant, and that the subject, whatever it was, was hateful to him.

When Thursday came, Miss Bell loitered in the breakfast-room, as we left it, that she might speak to me alone. It had happened that I had had no chance to talk with her by herself, since the day I took her message so unconsciously to George Rossiter. This morning she said, hurriedly, and careful that we should not be overheard, "Do you know why Mr. Fisher is going to the meeting to-night, the ratification meeting?" I had even forgotten it was Thursday. But I felt guilty at the moment, as one does when he has a secret. Of course if he were going I knew why. But I stumbled, as a man with a secret does, and showed her, merely by my manner, that I had a secret, and perhaps that it was a secret that I did not understand. I said: "Is he going? I did not know it till you told me."

"He is going," said she. "He is determined to go. And he will not tell me why. Yet it would be much better that he should not go. He never does go, and that makes me think—" here she paused, "that he knows he ought not to go. You men are just so obstinate," she said, trying to laugh, but with her eyes full of tears, which made her more charming than ever. Then she looked me square in the eye. "And you cannot tell me why he goes."

Of course I could tell her; and, whether I ought to tell her or no, Mary Bell with her eyes full of tears could have turned me round her finger. I told her what the crazy woman had said to me.

Her only answer was: "I was afraid it was that. So William Salter is to make the speech. Ungrateful hound!" Then, as if it were another subject, "Mr Fisher will never take me with him. Will you—"

There was an instant when I was exquisitely happy that she had asked me for such a service, but she made no pause at that instant, nor indeed thought that I was fool enough to be deceived. She simply showed me what a fool I was as she finished it.

"Take me and Cordelia Grattan with you. We cannot go alone. But we can all have one of the carriages." Carriages, to be sure, as if it would not have been better to have walked with her twenty miles, than to have sailed in Cleopatra's barge with Cordelia Grattan and her! Why should Cordelia Grattan and her millions come in every-where? This was the thought which passed through my mind. But, alas! it met the other thought that, if we were to walk to the meeting alone, George Rossiter might overtake us.

To the ratification meeting accordingly we went, taking very sedulous care that John Fisher should not know we were going. But, indeed, an ominous silence hung over the whole day, which was quite enough to show me that there was a secret, if in my own private duty I had not known it perfectly well. In that house, of all the houses in Tamworth— in that house, where every preparation for the election had been begun, not one word was said of the great meeting which virtually crowned the work, which even decided by its success or failure how the work was to end. We made our arrangements so as not to interfere with Mr. Fisher's, and about this there proved to be no difficulty, as he had made his so as not to interfere with ours. We arrived at the hall rather early and so had tolerably good seats in the gallery, which was reserved for ladies and their friends. But the building soon filled up, and was crowded, except on the platform, before any person appeared there. To my disgust, George Rossiter saw us from below and came and joined us where we sat, quite unconscious that I could have wrung his neck, had the customs of society and the instructions of the decalogue permitted.

A good band was playing when we went in, and continued to play until the meeting began. But I do not think any person listened for an instant to the music. It filled the office of music well, if it be true that we are quite unconscious of the best. We were all watching to see who was there, and wondering if this or that person were not there. Just at the hour appointed, half-past seven, from a mysterious side passage, the committee and dignitaries filed in upon the platform. The ladies of my party watched them with a good deal of feeling—now of admiration, generally of ridicule, and sometimes of scorn. " Little John Ryder; he does Ward III." "Really, Mary, there is Theodore Gross! Who would have thought it? Buttons at the front. Mary, he is looking for you." " Col. Stothers! See Col. Stothers! They ought to cheer Col. Stothers." The Colonel had not been at a ratification meeting since the Town Hall was built, and did not know the intricacies of the platform. When he was dragged well to a prominent seat at the front, the audience, sooner of course than the ladies, took the idea, and cheered him vigorously. He had earned his cheer by withdrawing in favor of Dr. Witherspoon, who appeared a moment after, and was cordially received in his turn.

All this time the band was playing "Hail to the Chief," as loud as it could play, but it seemed as if no one, excepting a dilettante visitor like me, knew or cared that they were not playing the "Dead March in Saul."

Mr Fordyce, who was their Member of Congress, presided, and presided very well. He spoke at length on the exigency, which he really thought to be of the utmost importance to the people, so that he could say so without lying, or any rhetoric analogous to lying. He said that on another occasion he should like to talk to them on national politics, and he hoped that they would give him an opportunity. "But not to-night." He hoped that to-night Democrats and Republicans and Third Party Prohibitionists or First Party Greenbackers were together to join in establishing permanently the good government of Tamworth, which they had only partly won by the magnificent victory of last year. That victory had been welcomed by the whole country. Once and again he had been congratulated on it in Washington.

At this point in Fordyce's speech, Mary Bell seized Cordelia Grattan's arm. "There's that viper, William Salter!"

"Where?" said the other, eagerly.

"The second man in the row behind him. The man with something red in his button-hole. I wonder the earth doesn't open under him."

I was glad to be thus far prepared for the drama. Fordyce was going on with his explanation of last year's victory, and what must be done to complete it. He made a very good picture of what his father and their fathers did, not thirty years ago, when Tamworth was not; when there

was then " only a possible Tamworth, a Tamworth of the
future ; and for its present, ladies and gentlemen, only a
swamp which no man could cross, and a creek which no
man could sail in and a tangle of cotton-wood which no man
could see through. What did my father and your fathers
do then? Did they array themselves in two camps, because
some of them came from Europe and some were born in
America? No ! They hewed at the same tree, and they
lugged the same log. Did they settle, the Democrats on
one side the creek and the Republicans on the other? No !
My father split shingles for a man whose politics he hated,
and that man cooked the coon which they both ate for their
dinner.

"And I will not ask, gentlemen—and ladies, for I see
we are honored by the presence of ladies ; I will not ask,
Where were the people who are opposing us this week? I
do not know. I know they were not here. I know they
were not honorably building up the best interests of this
place or of any place. They were somewhere; where they
did not learn the lesson of the pioneer. They did not learn,
and they do not know, that every good citizen owes his first
endeavor to the town he lives in, that it may be wholesome,
pure, clean, and healthy ; that it may be a pleasure and a
blessing to live in it ; that its children and youth shall not be
led into temptation ; that its men and women shall live under
equal laws. When you have cared for this, gentlemen and
ladies, then, and not till then, may you adorn your palaces
and improve your gardens, may you take the luxury of your
libraries, and the recreation of your music. Your first duty
is for the fair and pure and just government of the town in
which you live."

Mr. Fordyce had struck his key-note well. Clipsham followed him, who was, as it happened, a special favorite at that moment, with these people. He had just returned from his wedding-tour. There was some banter, which I did not understand, about a speech he should have made the year before, which he had made in the wrong place. The audience understood it, and cheered him heartily as he came forward. His speech, like Fordyce's, was on the general matter of the importance of good city government. A man named Jones followed, who had the finally-revised list of the School Committee and of the Aldermen, and it was his business to explain it and account for its omissions. He did this in a hemming and hawing sort of way from different papers he had, very badly arranged. But it was interesting to see that his speech was received quite as cordially as was either of the two orations we had heard. Evidently he was a man whom everybody respected, and it was understood that what he and his committee had to say was not only nearly final but probably right. Evidently also some people were dissatisfied. And to Mary Bell's terror and Mrs. Grattan's they began to ask questions. These ladies thought that such questions were ill-bred and rude, and I observed that they always considered that the men who asked them were morally wrong, and wished to break up society from its foundations. Women are Monarchists of nature. They only try the wild experiment of Democracy, as the brave Peruvian princes mounted on Pizarro's stray horses, to show that they can do this also. I tried, without much success, to re-assure my friends, and to explain that these inquirers had their rights in a public meeting, and, if such questions were not put and answered, there was no use in our being there.

"I never said there was any use in our being here," said
Mary Bell rather tartly. "I never thought there was.
But, as the meeting was to be, I wanted to come." Had
Napoleon governed that city, by the simple appointment of
a Provost-marshal, and the proclamation of martial law,
both of them, at the outset, would not have been displeased.

A "Provost-marshal" is a ruler of a city who does what
he chooses, and "Martial Law" is the law which permits
him to do so.

But I on my side with Mrs. Grattan, and Mr. Rossiter on
his side with Miss Bell, explained again, as well as we
could, that, if republican government meant anything, such
interruptions or questions were not only to be permitted but
desired. How could we ratify that which we did not explain? To which Mrs. Grattan said in reply, "There
should be some one to say what shall be done and what shall
not be done. That was the way my grandmother put it, or
I believe it was hers. It was in George the King's time,
anyway." To which all I could say was that her grandmother's mother was a sad Tory, and that she appeared to be
another. To which she did not reply. It was clear enough
that the people on the platform were neither discouraged
nor displeased. When a demand more trenchant than usual
was put in form, "Why did you drop Pasteboard Tom?"
you would see an intelligent smile pass from one of the
dignitaries to another, as much as to say: "I told you
you would get into trouble if you interfered there." But the
community has in it an element of Kentucky blood, and, as
my friend the Boss had told me, it was trained both to the
town meeting of New England and to the barbecue of Kentucky, blended together in all their wild and native frank-

ness. It was interesting and edifying to me, to see how simply and frankly and courageously the members of the final committee on nomination took these interpellations. They were never taken by surprise. Indeed, they almost courted questions. It was as if you had brought five "catchers" together on the platform, and invited all the "pitchers" of the town to try their hand with them. The moment one reply was made they would look round, almost eagerly, as if to court another question. When it came, the man who was to reply knew it was his question, and did not hesitate an instant. Nor did any one else interfere with him. Thus, to that dangerous question about Pasteboard Tom :

"Mr. James B. Stimson, of Ward III, is the person alluded to, I believe. If he is here, he will tell us why he is called 'Pasteboard Tom.' I do not myself know. I do know why I voted against him in committee ; and I suppose other gentlemen agreed with me. He was absent from four meetings of the Council last summer without a pair. He has very curious views on the pavement of N Street, for he voted for it after Tibbles bid for the contract, when he had voted steadily against it before. I thought, if he wanted to go after buffalo again this summer, he had better go."

Mr. Stimson's friend had taken very little by his motion, for this answer was received with laughter and cheers. But the committee was not always so fortunate.

Quite a large man, dressed much more carefully than the most, stood up on the end of a settee, and when one interpellation had ended, with great dignity said :

"Mr. Chairman"—

All other interpellants stopped ; there was a hush, and then a general cry of "Green! Green! Green!"

The chairman recognized Dr. Green with great courtesy.

"Many of the oldest residents are greatly displeased that the name of our esteemed friend, Silas Backup, is dropped from the school committee. I have nothing to say against the very able names on the list put into my hands. They are very good men. But Mr. Backup has experience—long experience. And I shall vote for him. Many others will vote for him." And he sat down.

The committee-man whose business it was stepped forward—this time without a particle of arrogance or of flippancy. All the committee had the greatest respect for Mr. Backup, it seemed—"their venerable friend," as he called him. He remembered, himself, and he was no longer young, when Mr. Backup examined him in geography in the old school-house. But there seemed to be an impression, perhaps he might say among the younger teachers, that some rotation in office was desirable, and as Mr. Backup had been in service, as teacher and afterwards as committee-man, now for twenty-nine years, a majority of the committee had reluctantly determined to replace the name by that of a younger man—Col. Wintress, of the Fort Plain district. The Fort Plain people had had no member on the committee for five years. But he was instructed to say that, if any dissatisfaction was expressed, the committee wished to refer the change to the meeting, and he asked the chairman to submit it.

"The man is an old fool," said Cordelia Grattan hastily to me. "The book-sellers twist him right round their fingers."

The chairman stepped forward to put the vote, amid rival shouts of "Backup!" "Backup!" and "Wintress!"

"Wintress!" I observed that the gentlemen on the platform generally refrained from voting. But the show of hands gave the place to the "old fool" of Mrs. Grattan's vocabulary, three to one.

"Somebody has to be sacrificed," said Rossiter. "If they really wanted to carry Wintress in, they should have nominated Backup, and had Wintress named from the floor."

The ladies, meanwhile, now that they took the notion of the interpellations, were very much interested, and wanted more. Alas! I was afraid that there would be one too many. But I think that even Mary Bell had forgotten her fears in the interest of this drama, as new to her as to Mrs. Grattan.

The people, however, had their little victory over a committee, which, on the whole, they thoroughly confided in, and were not disposed to carry the interpellations farther. "Shut up!" "Oh, be still!" "Question, Question, Question!" began to interrupt people who asked about candidates, and the interest was decidedly flagging, when, on the platform itself, the terrible William Salter stepped forward, and, to the chairman's surprise, clearly enough addressed him.

"The traitor," said Cordelia Grattan, and for the first time I knew that she knew there was some sort of danger connected with him. I turned to look at Mary Bell. She was no longer leaning forward with eager curiosity. She was resting back, as if faint, on the seat, as pale as the white rose she wore.

Mr. Salter then said, in an easy speech, almost like the address of a lawyer of the first rank, who by some accident finds himself patronizing a judge in an inferior court, that he had waited till the meeting, which he highly respected, should have determined the details of the ticket. The ticket bore many names which he valued. For some of the persons named on it he should vote. But the time had come when the hollow character of the nomination should be exposed, and he was there to express the feelings of those who wished to expose it. Here was all the form of a Town Meeting. Here was all the machinery of a Committee. What was it for? It was all to register the decisions of one man. In a work-shop which he need not name, this man instructed his vassals how they should vote.

"You shut up!" "Speak for yourself!" "Hold your jaw!" "Hush! Hush! Hush! let him go on!"

This from the audience. Mr. Salter was not fluttered. Not he! He said that was the sort of freedom of speech, they would observe, which the myrmidons of their master believed in and permitted. But this was not a gagged meeting, and he was not a man to be frightened. He was saying, when these hirelings broke in, that the whole thing was cut and dried, either in the counting-room on Z Street, or in the palace whose festivities were the marvel of the whole West, or in one or another lodge room, so secret that even an Argus-eyed press could not tell us where their dark councils were held. From these conclaves came out certain decrees, certain instructions, which the people of Tamworth were that night called upon to approve.

By this time there was a dead silence. The attack was wholly unexpected, and there was an intense curiosity to know what it meant and what it was coming to. John Fisher, who was on the very front of the platform, sitting on the outer chair of a row which faced the speakers, so that his profile was before the most of the assembly, sat perfectly still, looking straight in Salter's face. He was, perhaps, a little pale. Salter never turned that way.

He went on, growing nervous, I thought, as he spoke. He never called a cheer, or any token of sympathy from the crowd, but, from first to last, commanded absolute attention. He tried to ridicule John Fisher's displays of wealth, but no one laughed. He asked why he did not put his servants, footmen and coachmen as he called them, in livery, and suggested the colors, "black and blue," but no one laughed. I think he was wounded by the failure to draw the help of any of the assembly, perhaps of some on whom he had relied. I think he fired his last shot before he meant.

"And who is this English lord, whose army of body-servants, not in livery, carry his messages, and do their master's will? Whence comes this wealth, which has paid this band to play 'Hail to the Chief,' when he stepped upon this platform, which pays for the roses which the school children throw under his feet? Where does the treasure come from with which he suborns the press, and compels the unwilling scribblers to support, not him, oh no! he is always in the background, but the Slaves of the Lamp and the Ring?

"I will tell you, gentlemen. It is not a week since I came at the secret. For you and I cannot do such things. If poor, mean William Salter, if I should go to a pawnbroker's with a copper ring, and tell him it was gold, and if an ignorant boy took it from me and paid me for it, I should go to the penitentiary. Poor Mike Flaherty was sent to the County-house last week on a less offense. But when John Fisher wants money, his character is above suspicion! When John Fisher's bank account is short, he sends the carriage and servants and bids Madame go to the money-lenders! And Madame takes a pinchbeck gewgaw which no man here would give his daughter, and, because it is John Fisher's jewel, the poor boy whom she bids pays her I know not how many thousands upon it. And when the fraud is exposed, does John Fisher go to the penitentiary? Not much, gentlemen! He comes to this meeting and asks you to vote his ticket. But you will not do it. You will tear it to flinders!"

And, like a prophet, he rent the offending paper into shreds and threw them from him in scorn.

Not one cheer, not one word of applause, however. Salter was disconcerted, and said what I think he did not mean to. "There is Mr. Niederkranz. His boy lent the money. There is John Fisher. Ask either of them if what I say is not true."

Then there was, in one corner, not cheers, but clapping and stamping and pounding of canes. There was a general standing up all over the Hall, to see what would come next. There was a scuffle in one corner, and an excited man with a red head leaped with some difficulty upon the platform from the back of a settee.

The chairman, pale and surprised, called the meeting to order, insisted that people should sit down, while the red-haired man, held back by one or two of the Committee, was shaking his fist across the platform at Mr. Salter's face. This dumb show amused the crowd. There were one or two cries of "Hear him! Hear him!"

So soon as there was any return to silence, I heard Mary Bell say to Cordelia Grattan, "Why, it is Jan Hooft, my Dutch wire-drawer. What in the world has he to do with that viper?"

"Hush, Hush!"

Hooft was still shaking his fist. "I dort I would tell dem

vot she did mid de money, you black-horned, black devil! She come mit de money to Maurice Witt, when him vader was dying and you sent de sheriff to put him on de sidewalk. Dat was de first time I seed dem horses you toll on. She paid your man de money, twelve hundred dollar and dirty-two, mit seven cents more, and she paid fifty-two cents do de sheriff for de summons, and de sheriff gave dem cents to my Marie, coz he said it was blood money, you hund, you blackguard, blackguard, dat's what dey call him!"

And, greatly relieved, Jan Hooft rushed again toward Salter, but was stopped on his way. The whole assembly howled with delight; some hoping, perhaps, for a personal encounter. "Three cheers for Jan Hooft!" And they gave them with a will. All this time, the poor chairman was pounding and gesticulating. I do not think many persons noticed, as I did, that the man whom Cordelia Grattan pointed out to me as Niederkranz, irreproachably dressed, by the way, in full evening dress, was stepping across the backs of settees and reached the platform.

Mr. Salter had alluded to him by name.

Other people saw him, and cried, "Niederkranz, Niederkranz!" And this hushed the tumult more than the chairman. I looked, not at him, but at Mary Bell. She was ghastly pale. I begged her to leave the hall, but she hushed me, crowding her fingers tight upon my arm.

"Mr. Niederkranz!" said the chairman.

The old gentleman spoke slowly, but very clearly. "The speaker called my name. I will not call him my friend. He said something of a necklace which Mrs. Fisher left in our safe; and that we loaned her a trifle, confidentially, for which she chose to leave the necklace as collateral.

It is all true.   Does the gentleman think he has a monopoly
of lending money for interest?   He is mistaken if he does.
When the proper time came, she sent us the money, and the
necklace, which is of priceless value to her and to her friends,
was returned to her.   Is there more of the private business
of my firm, which Mr. Salter wishes to bring before this
meeting?"

But Salter was not there.   I had seen him take his hat
as soon as Jan Hooft was hustled from the platform.   One
or two voices called, "Salter, Salter!"   and the chairman
said, perhaps with a satirical turn, "Will Mr. Salter come
forward?"   But there was no William Salter.   Every one
was talking to every one else.   "The incident was exhaust-
ed," as the French say.   With some difficulty the chairman
pounded and screamed through a vote, confirming the nominations, and pledging support at the polls.

And so the meeting was over.

CHAPTER XIX.

NONE of us in the carriage, as we drove home, knew
how much the others knew.   There was, therefore,
a certain chill over the conversation.   I noticed, even before
we left the gallery, that Mary Bell's face was no longer pale.
It was blazing with color.   Had this Mr. Rossiter said anything to her to excite her?   He led her to the carriage, and
left us there.

"Shall we not look for Mr. Fisher?" said I, before the
carriage started.

"No," said Miss Bell promptly, "he will be better pleased if we take care of ourselves, and leave him to come when

he is ready." So we entered the carriage, and gave the order for home.

After a painful pause, I ventured to say, "A scene indeed. Did you guess what was coming?"

"Only half," said Mary Bell, "and that half I did not dare tell you."

"Did he know it was coming?" said Mrs. Grattan.

"Yes," said I, "I gave him the warning myself." And then I told her what I knew.

"Brave creature!" said Cordelia Grattan. "Shall we ever understand him? Certainly we shall never understand his wife. Pawning jewels for money! When if she had asked him for a million, he would have given it to her."

Mary Bell said nothing.

When we came to the door, John Fisher was standing there. He had arrived before us.

"So you saw our little melodrama," he said, coolly, as he handed the ladies from the carriage. "Virtue triumphant, and vice defeated. Come up to supper; Mrs. Edwards will be raging."

"Is the man iron?" said Cordelia Grattan to me. And so we passed into the breakfast-room, as for some reason, not known to me, the room was called in which we generally met, just before bed-time, for such refection as Mrs. Edwards thought best fitted for that fifth meal of the day.

Were you happily following the pages of Dumas or of Dickens, reader of mine, you would know what the entertainment on this occasion was. But, as you have learned to your sorrow, this author is more reserved than they.

Fisher served us himself, and affected to be even gay.

But he was not, and we all knew him so well that we knew that he was not. Still, he would not " go back" on what he had said at the house door. So soon as he saw us well engaged in the conflict with hunger and thirst he took up the same theme.

" You had all tried to forewarn me, but Cassandra herself could not have told us, I think. What I am to say to my wife, I am sure I do not know. If she brings us into scrapes, her allies certainly bring us out again."

I said that Jan Hooft, if that were his name, would certainly take any prize for oratory, even over the head of the famous Mr. Clipsham.

Once more Miss Bell's face flushed crimson, as I had seen it in the gallery at the hall, and as I never saw it before. I was opposite to her so that I could not but see this, and for a moment I thought she would rise and leave the table. But she staid and pretended to sip her chocolate. " She is iron, too," I said to myself. Fisher felt, I think, that he had said all that needed to be said, and so led the talk into a discussion of the rights and wrongs of the episode, by which Col. Wintress was ousted from his place on the school committee, and that " old fool" was put in again.

" I told them," said he, " to have Wintress named from the floor. But they said I was no manager, and undertook to arrange things their own way."

Cordelia Grattan told him that Mr. Rossiter had made the same suggestion.

CHAPTER XX.

MRS. FISHER did not appear at breakfast the next morning. Nor did she appear before we left the house. And I observed that the children, who were generally quite willing enough to discuss the scraps of local news, and who were wildly interested in the canvass, which was indeed, by this time, the centre of every one's thought, I observed, I say, that the children made no allusion to the scenes of the night before. This was the more striking, because Bedford had been on the floor with some of his comrades, and had seen with his eyes and heard with his ears.

It was again one of those days when there was no question what we should do. It was what was called "Harvest Day," a sort of anticipation of Thanksgiving, which had been intercalated for the purpose of inventing an autumn holiday for the school-children.

"This year," said Mary Bell, "it is all nonsense. For they had their parade and holiday the day when we laid the corner-stone. But the 'custom was introduced,' as the newspapers say, some five years ago, by an enterprising high-school teacher. Your purists would say that we cannot introduce a custom. But we know better, and have done it. And these very children in this house think there has been a harvest day, and that school-rooms have been decorated with wheat and barley and rice and sugar-cane, ever since " Adam delved and Eve span."

"Where shall we take Mr. Mellen, Cordelia? Of course we must go to the High School, for Edgar speaks. But for the other schools, shall it be kindergarten, introductory, primary, secondary-primary, preparatory, grammar, grammar-technical, technico-classical, classical or secondary? Shall we go to the Logan School, the Harrison, the Meriwether, the Tennyson, the Johnson, the Stubbs, or the La Salle?"

It was agreed that we should spend an hour at one of the kindergartens, not so much, so far as I could see, for anything which we were to learn about education, but because Agnes Fitch, the teacher, was "so pretty, and so nice." Then we were to do two hours at the Meriwether School, because the children were all Norwegians, and Dutch, and Germans, and Bohemians, and of every other name and nationality under heaven, except that of the country to which they all owed allegiance. Then, promptly at twelve, the carriage was to be at the side-door of the Meriwether, and we were to take two hours at the High School that we might hear Edgar speak in the French dialogue in which Miss Bell had been coaching him.

Like many other men, who have themselves spent a good deal of time in teaching the young, and so in "getting up" exhibitions, I had not felt much enthusiasm about all this, and certainly I came down to breakfast with no intention of going to primary, middle or secondary. I had my morning work to do, and it never occurred to me that my presence was necessary at either of these solemnities.

But I observed on the instant, that I was not to exercise any choice on this occasion. So far as I remembered for every other party of the endless series in which the household was involved, I had always been asked, in form, whether I wished to go or no. But here my wish was taken for granted. Or rather it was taken for granted that I should go whether I wished it or not. This was so evident from the first, that I did not even struggle. I was prevented, fortunately, from committing myself. And I did not intimate, by a wink or by shrug, that five hours spent on crowded school settees, at school exhibitions, were not for me the very happiest hours of my life.

What surprised me even more was to find, when we met at the front door at quarter of nine, that John Fisher, dressed as for a gala day, was of the company.

"Mr. Mellen, I must put you in trim," said Cordelia Grattan. "Really, you know, you are very nice, but you do not look as if anybody took an interest in you. I must give you one of my carnations."

And she pinned one upon my coat. I was forced to confess that I had not known that we were expected at the exhibition.

"They are all red-letter days here," said she, in an undertone, looking at Fisher, who was giving his hand, at the carriage, to Miss Bell. "Whatever else is neglected in this house, any honor that can be paid to the schools is rendered."

And he took up her remark, as we all entered the carriage and started. "Yes," he said, "any man who really wants to keep in the ebb and flow of life will be wise if he keeps the run of the schools. You learned people make a great fuss about what you call your charities. If you could really get at the English of the thing, it would appear that in the public-school teachers, by and large, through the country, you have a staff of intermediaries between the comfortable classes and those in need, such as none of your charity machinery will manufacture in many years. My Miss Mather and that nice Mrs. Philbrick are at the Logan, and Sarah Plaisted—and your friend, Mrs. Grattan, the girl that squints, this Miss Fitch—these are all teachers, Mellen, and they are all sisters of charity. They know where the shoe pinches, and they know how to help, and where. Why, Sarah Plaisted showed me a drawer full of jaunty neckties, which she keeps ready, so that no Mike, or Bernard, or Jack, or Tom, of the crew, may be mortified because he does not look as well as the best. And that favorite subject of your novelists, the widow supported by her children's exertions, when she exists, which is not often, always knows the "teacher" and the "teacher always knows her."

"Oh, dear!" he said laughing, "I wish I could jerk out the word 'teacher,' as the little pirates do. Half of them cannot remember the teacher's name. And when they struggle to be mannerly to me, they invariably call me 'Ma-am,' instead of 'Sir.'

"But I am not going to the exhibition," he added, "because these good people are good almoners. I am going because the schools are the centre of the whole concern. They exist, by the goodness of God, and are a great deal better than one could imagine they would be. Your gilt-edged people are beginning to sniff at them, and the bigots would be very glad to tear them to pieces, and shirks and do-nothings are always trying to ruin their own children by stealing their education from them. They take them from school and send them where they can earn wages. All decent people, Mellen, who want the commonwealth to endure, should do what you and I are doing, and when a chance comes, show an interest in the affair."

I had to confess to him, as I had to Mrs. Grattan, that I had come because the rest came. "All right," said he, "so you count one on the platform."

One always picks up something now at a public school, and, once in the whirl of the exhibitions, I was entertained. But the interesting thing of all was to see how many friends —one would say intimate friends—John Fisher had among the children. He would nod to them, and they grin at him. He occasionally slipped a lozenge, by much stealth, into the hand of a little tot; once or twice he crossed the room to speak to a boy or girl, and, in general, he showed much more interest in the children as children than in the examinations, which showed how many facts, of more or less import, had been drilled into them. As we went from room to room, there would be an evident buzz of satisfaction wherever he appeared. As we went from the kindergarten to the older grammar school, I congratulated him upon this. I told him it was the most satisfactory reward a man could have for such a loyal interest as he had expressed.

"It keeps me young," said he. "That is the best reward. But, in truth," he added, with serious pleasure, "Mrs. Grattan, there, calculated the other day that there are twenty-two thousand young people in this world who have a right to stop me in the streets, because in these fifteen years past I have held some personal relation toward them in these schools. I have signed their diplomas, or, perhaps, presented them when some one else signed them, or I have given the bouquets, or they have had their dance on our green, or something has correlated us, as your pundits would say. Yes; that is a pleasure to a man like me, who believes that man is a gregarious animal."

A scene in the Meriwether grammar-school illustrated this "correlation," and really brought the tears to his eyes.

So soon as we arrived, we were received with ceremony and state, as if we had been admitted to a private show of the Royal Academy in London. Handsome boys of fifteen, with the orange and white, which proved to be the colors of the schools, blazing at their button-holes in orange blossoms and marigolds, escorted us up the stairs. Two head marshals, with ornamented batons, bearing the same colors, gave them directions where Mr. Fisher should sit and where the ladies, and where poor I, who was the inferior among all. John Fisher, I need not say, was among the highest dignitaries. His seat was actually next the master's throne. The girls who were in the highest class were prettily dressed in uniform, which showed how the homes were 'subordinated' to the school. Every girl wore orange and white in some form. But it was, alas, too late in the season for the white frocks which belong to school girls, and in which they look their prettiest.

The great hall, to which we arrived by painful climbing, one of the kind which Dr. Holmes calls a "High-story-call" hall, was crowded to the last corner. Dignitaries of both sexes were on the platform. Below, the favored seats were filled by ladies, among whom Miss Bell and Mrs. Grattan had "reserved seats," which were the grandest of all. Seats further back, or on the sides, were filled with men, among whom was I, and it was clear enough that all sorts of people were making a holiday of the occasion. I was sure that there was many a man who would not have left his work for any less occasion than to hear Margaret sing or John speak at the exhibitions. As for dress, there was nothing in color or fabric to distinguish these people from the dons on the platform.

And so we went on through the programme. It is always new and it is always old. For me I always cry my eyes out on such an occasion; there is something in the fresh voice of girls or of boys which compels the tears, even if the singing of the words shows, beyond a doubt, that the sentences have been committed to memory. And when they sing together, there is a tenderness which wholly upsets me.

We were nearly done, when we came to one of the last of what the newspapers call " numbers " or " events." It was a trio sung by three girls, perhaps fourteen years old, at the piano. One of them, a pretty blonde, of features distinctly Dutch or German, sang with that sort of passion which has seemed to me most often to sweep singers away, as if, at least, they were less under the sway of the machinery of music than other artists are under the technicalities of their art. Anyhow, this child lost memory of the place and the audience, and sang her part in this hymn as if none but the good God heard her. And in the triumphant close, as the three sang together, her voice rose above the rest, as if it must rise. The whole assembly was hushed to absolute silence, and when the song was finished, whole seconds passed by, with the dead, still hush upon us all, before there swooped down upon the stillness the thunders of applause.

Quite without a hint, and I am sure, without any fore-thought, the girl who was the head of the school, who had a wreath in her hand, prepared for I know not what, crossed to the piano and put it on the pretty singer's head.

The child blushed, faltered, half smiled, half cried, grew pale, and then very prettily ran forward, down the steps, to her father, who was in the first row of men on one side. He rose and kissed her, patted her forehead prettily and took the garland in his hand. As he rose, I recognized him at once, and so did half the assembly.

It was Jan Hooft, the Dutch worker in wire, whose speech had come in so effectively the night before.

He bent down and kissed her again, and then fearlessly led her across the front of the stage, up the steps to the school-master's throne, and, before John Fisher knew it, the girl had placed the laurel on his head!

Of course, in an instant, he seized it and had it in his hand. But the whole company knew the story of the night before, and every one was clapping with all his might, if he were not waving his handkerchief. Every one who knew Jan Hooft told his name, and the thing gave every one a chance to ex-press pent-up enthusiasm for him and for his friend.

So it was, that I think I was almost the only person who saw a bit of by-play in this queer, mediæval scene. I turned, of course I turned, to see what Miss Mary Bell was doing or was thinking. Again her face was flushed with the intense blaze with which it had flushed the night before. She seemed all quivering with emotion. And, as I wondered, the girl, the singer, who roused all this emotion, turned from her father, passed to Miss Bell's seat, and flung herself into her arms as she might have into her mother's. This scene, however, was unnoticed by the assembly. As I say, they were clapping and waving, while Fisher and Hooft stood shaking hands and talking eagerly. Only I, who always watched Miss Bell if I could watch her, knew what was passing with her, and wondered what this fascinating woman had to do with this remarkable child. Hooft and Fisher indeed, could not have heard a word which either said. It was all dumb show. And in a minute, a chair had been found for the wire-drawer by John Fisher's side, and he was compelled to sit in it, that so the performance might go on. Meanwhile, Mary Bell soothed and petted the girl; kissed her again and again, and finally persuaded her to take her seat again, her own cheeks blazing with crimson all the time.

No school was allowed to hold its audience more than two hours. For it was understood that the members of the committee and other officials must attend at several exhibitions in succession. We left with the others, found the carriage, and drove to the High School, where one of our own boys was to speak.

But, if I expected to have a word privately with Mary Bell, as we left the school-house and went to the carriage, I was disappointed.

CHAPTER XXI.

[ANOTHER INTERPOLATED CHAPTER. MR. MELLEN'S MEMOIRS ARE FULL, BUT THERE ARE SOME POINTS WHICH HE, FOR SOME REASON, DID NOT CARE TO ENTRUST TO WRITING.]

AS they drove from the High School after the last speeches had been spoken and the last diplomas given, it proved that John Fisher had an errand in the town, in carrying out which he needed Mrs. Grattan's judgment. After a little discussion, it was arranged, therefore, to Mr. Mellen's great joy—though he had, of course, no voice in these plans—that, at the corner of Fremont Avenue and La Salle Street, these two should leave the carriage and take a street-car for their shopping, while Miss Bell and Mr. Mellen rode home together, and were to announce that the other two would be at home within ten or fifteen minutes.

Lucky Mr. Mellen—to ride home with her and no one else, with ten good minutes to say what he would, and no possibility that she should escape him, even if she wished it.

Alas, he did not use his time for the very best. At least he thought so afterwards.

He did not mean to lose a moment's time. He began with the adventure at school.

" That girl is another Jenny Lind, if one may trust the Jenny Lind pictures. She came to you as if you were her sister. How have you known her, and what is the mystery of all this? I have half the secret of the necklace; can you not tell me the whole?"

"Secret! Why do you call that a secret, which was proclaimed before two thousand people?"

"Because I think it was not proclaimed. I do not believe, and I do not think you believe, that the two thousand people went away much better informed than they came." And Mr. Mellen added with some hesitation, because he was in doubt how far he had better go:

"And I supposed; yes, I suppose now that if you chose you could tell—well, that at least you could tell, if you wished, more of the interior of Jan Hooft's house than you did. I thought so, even when we were talking at breakfast, and since the girl kissed you so eagerly and passionately, why, I think so more than ever."

Mary Bell smiled, but not with her engaging or fascinating smile. She smiled rather as if she forced herself to smile, and then she said, with a little flush:

"You thought I could tell, if I chose, Mr. Mellen. And what do you think I shall tell, if I do not choose?"

Mellen saw in a moment that he had gone too far. He had, in fact, put himself in the false position of a man who has to begin a critical conversation with an apology. But he made the apology like a man.

"I beg your pardon. But you spoil us, Miss Bell. You have been, as I tell you every day, my guide, philosopher, and friend, in the intricacies of this life, where I might stumble every day. You must not take it hardly if I try your good nature too far."

" Not my good nature," said she, not trying now to laugh or to pretend to any longer. " No, you may be sure that I will try to be good-natured. But my prudence, my discretion ; if you please, my wisdom—yes. Do not try them too far, if you please, for I am not sure of them myself in this matter, and I dare not say to myself at what moment they may give way."

Mellen would have said, had he dared, that she was the " wisest, virtuousest, discreetest, best," and the prudentest of women, as well as the most charming and to him the dearest.

But he did not dare. He did say, with some hesitation :

" I would have said, Miss Bell, had I any right to say so, and if I have not you must forgive me, that if any woman can trust her own judgment you can ; if any woman is apt to be prudent, you are. Surely, very few people would venture to advise you."

She was as pale now as he had seen her once before. And she did not look at him, but at the vacant cushion beside him, as she slowly answered :

" Yes, I have my secret, and, to be quite frank with you, I shall act on the rule you taught us the first day you were here : ' If you want your secret kept, keep it.' Whether I were wise to have such a secret, that is a different thing. But I am so glad you liked Minna Hooft. How could you help it, indeed ? You must ask Cordelia about her. Cordelia has watched her voice with great care, and has a right to be proud of it."

Mr. D'Israeli tells a story of Venetia in her childhood, that she said to her nurse, "I do not want to talk about butterflies ; I want to talk about widows." Had Mellen dared, he would have said, "I do not want to talk about Minna Hooft ; I want to talk about you, and tell you what a charming and noble woman you are, and how I wish I might say more."

But a man cannot always say what he wants to.

" She does you infinite credit," he said, not impatiently. "And, if for two or three years she has such guides, what may not be hoped for her? But tell me, Miss Bell, what is your method. How is it that your hand is in every hand ; that you counsel statesmen by John Fisher's intervention, that you lift Jan Hooft out of his miseries, close the dying lips of that poor creature I left you with last week, and, all the same, are the life of our house ; my ' guide and philosopher' ; nay, even poor Mrs. Fisher's protector. You ought to tell your pupil how all this is done."

There was not the least frivolous shadow over what he said. He said it, indeed, very eagerly. He meant what he said, though he wanted it to lead farther. And she could not— nay, she would not laugh it off as compliment.

" Oh, Mr. Mellen, you are asking for my autobiography. How I was educated and what came of it. If we shall ever take an Indian voyage together, there will be time for me to tell you. Seriously, if one means to do the duty next her hand, I fancy one finds no difficulty as to variety of life."

" I was not asking about variety of life. So far as I see, life has only too much variety. What I want to know is how to keep well the whip-hand on life as you do. You are never surprised. Pardon me, you never lose your temper. You never say a smart, sharp thing, even when you think it." He was going on to say, " You come into a room, and all is sunshine. You talk to a fool, and he becomes a man of sense." Nay, he would probably have said, "You are the most charming and lovable woman in the world, and you do not know it."

But she had no intention of letting his eulogy run into an unmanageable stage, and she interrupted him. Once more the conversation was skilfully landed in another hemisphere.

"Oh, you ask to many questions. And I am the last person to answer them. You must go to some of your great talkers for that. Is not that the good of your Grand Mémoires, in ten volumes, which you men find time to read, but I never. I look on those sets of books, 'Mémoires pour Servir,' and I wonder. But you; you are a scholar. I shall have an advantage when you come to the higher education again. Was it not you who quoted Madame de Genlis so skilfully to Miss Porter?"

Mellen held his ground, though he saw, perhaps, that she did not mean that he should.

"You know very well," he said, bravely, "that this is no matter of books. You know that I might go through some post-graduate courses, and that no professor could teach me what you can. You know, also—I am sure you do me that justice—that I am the last man in the world to talk compliment to you. You know I respect you too far—I wish I might say I admire you too far. I am grateful, now, for this chance of saying this while we are alone." And, if Mary Bell had let him go on, Mr. Mellen would have improved the minute he had left to go much further and say much more.

It will not do to say that his mind was absorbed in that one purpose. Minds are capable of carrying on many lines of "cerebration" at once. And, while he was saying all this, almost passionately, he was thinking, with equal passion, "Why does this infamous Thomas, on the box, drive these horses so much faster than they ever went before."

Miss Bell was pale. She was very attentive. She did not lose her self-possession. At the moment when he said "Alone"—when he had to pause—though for the least instant, for a mere differential of a second—she replied to him as if he had waited for an answer, and with no air of interrupting him.

"Indeed, Mr. Mellen, I do you full justice. Indeed, I am sure you have seen that we are friends, true friends. You said so within the minute, even when, in joke, you called me a philosopher, which we both know that I am not. Mrs. Grattan and I have been saying, only to-day, that we were glad you determined to stay into next week, because—well —because we were glad." There was a faint blush, as if she had trifled, and indeed she had. But he was to have no chance to take up his broken thread. "She is grateful—I am grateful—that there is one man who comes to this house who has not an axe to grind, who has no college to endow, no water-fall to develop, no city to found, no invention to explain. More grateful are we that this strange visitor pays us the first of compliments by treating us as if we were women of sense. Why, we had a man here who told Mrs. Grattan that orthography meant good spelling, and another told me that Mr. D'Israeli was the leader of the Tory party."

Not one chance did she give to Mr. Mellen, as she talked on. And probably she would have gone on with her illustrations, but,. at this moment, this Jehu Tom swept round the curve of the avenue, and drew up at the front door of the house.

Whether he would or no, Mr. Mellen had to step from the carriage and offer her his hand.

She mounted the steps rapidly before him. But he followed as rapidly. And, as she led the way across the ample hall, he said, with true courage, in a voice which could not but be heard :

"Pray do not go up-stairs. Step for a moment into the parlor."

She was too brave not to obey, and she turned. He led the way this time into an elegant satin-bedecked room of state, into which, in that house of comfort, nobody ever went, unless there was a great evening party. She followed him, as he asked her to do. She took the chair he offered her, quite behind the door. He was dead in earnest, it was easy to see that. He even closed the door as he passed it.

"You do not do me justice," he said. "You talk of Mrs. Grattan as if you and she were the same persons to me. I respect Mrs. Grattan. I admire her. But, with all her wealth, and with that ease which I suppose money brings with it, she does not work your miracles. If no one else tells you so, I will tell you so."

She looked on the carpet, and was thoroughly attentive now.

"I do not want to talk about Mrs. Grattan ; I want to

talk—well, about myself—and about Miss Mary Bell. And I want to talk of both together."

And here he tried to smile.

"I have asked you to come in here, because I have a favor to ask. You do not know me, I think—I hope—as well as I could wish that you knew me. I am sure that I know you—that is, I say so to myself every morning, and then every night I am sure that I know something of you which I never knew before. We are never alone, and that is the reason why I am so bold now. If you will believe——"

"Are you two here?" cried Mrs. Fisher, entering at this moment, from a little room, which was called the morning-room. "I have been roaming all round this empty house, to find some sort of society. One might as well live in a log-cabin. And here you have been talking temperance all the morning."

Mr. Mellen, who would have gladly thrown her out of the window, repressed himself so far as to say that they had but that moment come in; that they had come from the school exhibitions.

"I know that very well," said Mrs. Fisher, who had just before said she supposed something else. "I know where you all went. Mary told me. And, because I happened to breakfast up-stairs, no one could tell me in time. Because, I suppose, it is my pet pleasure of the year to go and hear these little things speak and sing, it had to be kept a dead secret from me. I came down just as you had gone, and found the house empty as usual."

Mr. Mellen hastened to say that a message from her maid gave Mr. Fisher the impression that she did not wish to go.

"I do not know what I said to Mary. My head was cracked with pain. I was not fit to sit up. And I should not have got up, but that everything goes wrong the minute I stay in bed fifteen minutes later than usual.

"Ah, Mr. Mellen, no man will ever understand what the care of a great household is, where one has, beside, the families of twelve hundred work-people to look after." And she sank, in her most helpless and confiding attitude, on the sofa by poor Mellen's side, and began with him, just as if she had never begun before, as if he were an entire stranger, and were wholly new to the story of her sufferings, her loneliness, and of what it was to be misunderstood or not understood at all.

"Now, take to-day," she said, in her most confidential tone. She was so confidential that Miss Bell rose, and said, " I will run up-stairs, and be ready for dinner. Cordelia will be here in five minutes, Mrs. Fisher, and your husband with her."

And poor Mellen—such is the fate of men in highly-civilized society—could not rush after her, and beg her to give him some chance to show her what man he was. He would have been so glad to say everything to her. Of what she had been to him already, and could be forever, if she would let him. And—such is destiny—instead of this, he must sit and share the wayward sorrows of his wayward hostess.

" Yes, Mr. Mellen," said Mrs. Fisher, so soon as Mary Bell had gone. " I was saying that this was one of the mornings when I felt specially well. I dressed myself with that feeling—you know what it is, dear Mr. Mellen—of exulting joy that I was in the world. Well, yes, I wanted to measure myself with the world. You understand me, I am sure, Mr. Mellen, though so few people do understand me. I felt as if poor I, also, could be of some use.

"And then, think of it. No, you cannot think of it. Without the experience of it, even you would not imagine it. To come down-stairs, ready for action, as I heard you say yesterday—or was it Mr. Rossiter who said it—to come down and find yourself quite left out and forgotten. That nobody wanted you, and all plans had been made without you."

She stopped, and suppressed a sob.

"Well, I shall be used to it some day, I suppose. Do not let us talk of that. Let us talk of something more important. You speak to-night, I think. May I go with you, dear Mr. Mellen? Interested as I am in everything which relates to the people, do not think that it is I who brings all the frivolity into this house. The girls—well, of course, Cordelia and Mary must spend their time as they will, and I am the last person to hinder them. But if I could, if—well, you know, dear Mr. Mellen, I will out with it. If it did not seem like flying in my poor husband's face, I would fill this house with such people as—well as you."

Mr. Mellen hastened to assure her that the society he had met in the house had been such as he had enjoyed and profited by.

"You are very kind. But I do think, sometimes, that if I ever had a well day—if I were not such a wretched wreck——"

At this moment they heard the front-door open, and John Fisher's voice, as cheery as if there had never been a cross to his life .

" All aboard ! Who's at home ? The prodigals have re- turned, and are all starving." And Mr. Mellen gladly left his companion, to meet Mr. Fisher and Mrs. Grattan in the hall.

CHAPTER XXII.

[MR MELLEN RESUMES THE PEN.]

MY visit was drawing to an end. I had engagements to speak in Illinois, and this life of luxury and variety could not last forever. Our great election was to come off on Tuesday, and I was to be one of many speakers at the final caucus of the friends of order on Monday night. On Saturday night the same senate which I had met once before, and but once before, at John Fisher's, was to meet again in his library for his last consultation.

" We ought to know the result to-night as well as if we waited for the slow marching of the vote," said Fisher, as we met in the cheerful room where the various chiefs of sec- tions were to appear. " Generally you do. With a can- vass as good as ours we know within fifty votes where we shall be, and we know about as well about the other side. But this year everything is confused, broken to pieces ; there are signs of a row in their camp."

He always spoke, as I have said, of " their " as he might have said " the Trojans," or " the Greeks," as if " They " were a proper name, and " their " its possessive case.

" But they know how to keep secrets, which is more than

we do. We wash our dirty linen in the most public ways we can find.

"Besides this, nobody knows what these third party people will do. ,Then there is this old greenback division, as if the question of paper or silver could be connected with the questions of purity or devildom. So that, in short, our most trusty prophets will be careful of their utterances this evening.

"I have met these, men when they were ready to wave their handkerchiefs and to hurrah when they came into the room, and again there are years when every man sits down at this conclave cross and blue, and says he is going to sell his house and move to Florence or Geneva for the rest of his life.

"But they never do move. They always stay here for one fight more. They stand up, like boxers, for one more round, and are sure, as Grant was at Donelson, that the other side must be as much demoralized as his own."

Our friends were very punctual; generally speaking they were in good spirits, and those who had bad reports to make took, in very good part, the chaffing of the others. As before, we had one representative of every ward. And the clock had hardly struck when the last man appeared.

At the moment, the whole party, who had been standing, took seats. It was clear that no moment was to be lost. I was the only outsider.

Silence fell over the company, all so gay in chatter but a moment before, and without the least formality, John Fisher said, turning to Ward I's man :

"How do we stand, Mr. Barnett?"

" Really," said Barnett, " it is much my old story. The athletic meeting was a great good fortune for us. We buried no end of hatchets. If you had time, you would like to know how important it was or seemed that the Glazier's nine should beat the Boot-tree men. Anyway it healed some very bad jealousies. I will not brag of my figures, but my reports give 'them' 473 votes ; say, to be sure, 480. We have 611, with some five chances for sick men and absentees. We are quite sure."

" How much cherry pectoral, John ? " This from the other side of the room. It was an old joke, referring to some occasion when Barnett had taken a sick voter to the polls in a carriage, and had, or was said to have, a bottle of cherry pectoral to stop his coughing when he was exposed to the air.

With such reports, now favorable, now unfavorable, we went on. I should not make a reader understand, if I tried to give the detail, which, indeed, I did not always understand myself. That complicated matter on the Hill was entirely healed over. Indeed we gained full two hundred votes from elegants who did not generally condescend to turn out at what they called ward elections. Dr. Witherspoon's candidacy was a very fortunate element, so far. We needed these votes on the general ticket, though in his own ward he would have been handsomely chosen without them.

But some hopes of the earlier meeting had been wholly blighted. Thus, in Ward VII, Varick had been quite sure, when we met before, that the Norwegians would insist on their own ticket, that the regular ticket which " They " sup-

ported would materially suffer from the defection, and that
if "We" could put up an absolutely faultless ticket we
might run in between the two factions of a broken enemy.
Varick had evidently favored the sedition of the Norwegians
to the best and the last. He had had Norwegian speakers
from Wisconsin, and circulated endless copies of flyers in
pure Norse. But, on Tuesday, his messengers had told him
that the whole bolt had caved in. The leaders of it, on
whom he had relied most, had sold out. One of them was to
have a billiard-room, rent free, and the other was to be
chosen for that ward on the school committee, where, till
this time, "They" had been willing to keep a very pure
and noble Catholic priest.

"That is all we have gained," said poor Varick, crest-
fallen. "This hound of a Knabe in the school-board instead
of dear old Father Managhan; and three councilmen—any
one of whom ought to be in the penitentiary."

Ward IX was as uncertain as the beginning of the fifth
act of a sensational drama. Whether the third party would
throw up its ticket at the end, and accept our men, or our
offer to take their nominations for street commission and gas-
inspector, or whether they meant to ruin the whole ward, and
let the enemy carry everything, no one would know until
Monday. Indeed, it all seemed to depend on the state of a
certain Tom Conner's digestion Monday noon. So at least
Wooster said, who reported for Ward IX. But the general
verdict was that if wheat rallied at Chicago before Monday,
Tom Conner would be all right and good-natured, and
would direct things sensibly. But if wheat continued to decline, Conner would be "mad" and would "break the
slate."

With many elements of doubt it was clear that we should carry the Mayor; we had a strong man with a backbone, who meant to succeed, himself, and had made a very favorable impression on the stump. Our canvass gave him 9,211 votes, and gave McCaull, who was on the other side, 7,800 in round numbers.

But with this stiff preponderence in the city, the wards were more doubtful. The wards had been skilfuly re-divided, the last time "'They" had the power. The Hill, which was dead against them, alone absorbed 3,000 of our votes, while a decent average ward had but 1,400 votes all told. Then there was another ward, four miles long and thirty rods across, which gave us 1,300 votes against 121. Similar contrivances had so bewitched the ward lines that we were sure of but four. It was clear that "'They" were sure of four in any contingency.

In the IVth, the VIIIth, and the XIIth, we could make no prophecy even now. We should need every vote in each of them. If we only won three we should have but seven wards against five, and every one felt that, with as compact an opposition as "'They" always made, this would be a very hollow victory.

CHAPTER XXIII.

I observed at breakfast that Mrs. Fisher's appetite was such as must encourage her friends. I sat next her, and her occasional comments on her food, as her plate was changed, or as some new dish was brought to her, made it impossible, even for the most unobserving, to be quite ignorant of her selections.

I was a little surprised, therefore, when, after an unusual term of silence, her second cup of coffee was brought to her, with some kidneys and mushrooms, which followed upon the broiled chicken she had been at work upon, to hear her say that she had lain awake all night with a raging neuralgic attack. "Every clock in this house did I hear strike every hour, Mr. Mellen," she said, pathetically. "And it seemed as if there were forty of them. And when that hateful cuckoo at the head of the stairs stepped out relentlessly, and yelled all the quarters at me, I wanted to rush out of the room and wring his neck for him. But I need not describe it, dear Mr. Mellen. You know what neuralgia is."

I said I was afraid I did not know. That if it was like what used to be called old-fashioned jumping toothache, I know very well what that was in old times, but that I had generally had courage enough to go to Dr. Handvise and let him pull the offender out. I found I had touched an irritable nerve.

"That's just what Cordelia there, and Mr. Fisher are forever saying to me. As if neuralgia were not one thing, and toothache wholly different. Mr. Mellen, believe me, I have not an unsound tooth in my head. Yet every night, now, since that miserable lawn party which I gave to the base-ball people, have I lain without a wink of sleep, while this shower of fire, I call it; shower of pain, you would call it, streams from my eyelids over my face on both sides. I have simply to bear it and bear it. 'Bear and forbear,' is

not that what you men say of women? I believe that is
what you think we are made for."

"Is there no sort of sedative?" said I, with all proper
sympathy. "Hops, bromine, or this new xylopogon from
Bolivia?"

"Mr. Mellen, if you have a friend you love, warn them
against such appliances, internal or external. Trust me,
for I know. No; tell your friend, if she is a woman, to
endure. Tell her to endure to the end," she added, in a
certain studied and rather artistic seriousness, to indicate
that she knew that the words came from the Bible. They
sounded well, and she repeated them. "Yes; let her endure to the end; there is no saying how soon that blessed
end may come;" this with a certain rapturous sigh, as if one
saw an open heaven before her.

I had been unsuccessful in both my ejaculations of sympathy, and tried another line : "You must lose strength,"
I said, "if you lose sleep, and how shall one talk of en-
durance, if one have no strength with which to endure?"

"I do not know. I do not know. There is resolution.
of course—resolution! Who shall say how far resolution
may carry one, if one truly resolves. If one truly resolves;
if one truly resolves."

This repetition, once or twice, of an axiom, is supposed
to give it a certain oracular power, as if one and another
nymph, according and sympathizing, flung it back, endorsed
"Seen and approved," in the glad echoes of their different
chancelries.

"If one truly resolves. If one truly resolves."

I hastened to say that for such resolution there needed a

balance of all the faculties, and that I hoped she might gain some help from a ride. The morning was beautiful; the air invigorating, and perhaps an hour or two's air-bath might prove an advantage.

"Oh, Mr. Mellen; I sometimes think that you men have neither hearts nor souls. You do not know what it is to feel; if to feel be to feel deeply, and to live—well, to live profoundly. My husband, there, is always saying what you do. 'Will not a ride do?' or, 'Would you not like a cup of tea?' or, 'Perhaps I can send you a slice of toast.' You are always prescribing physical remedies, when the difficulty is deeper down. It is a difficulty, Mr. Mellen, of that—well, we call it Life, because we have no better name for it, it has no name, and I ought not wonder that I cannot speak of it so that any one can understand me. But take an instance. Here am I. A common-place, every-day woman. Thousands of women are exactly like me; shop-girls, factory-girls, actresses, milliners, women on the prairies yonder, hoeing their husband's cabbages. We are all women, though we dress in one or another sort of finery, and lead different external careers. Still at heart we are women. So far we lead one life. I call it Life, because, you know, there is no better name for it. One day there will be, I hope. Or, rather, I suppose that one day we shall be able to name Life without speaking of it.

"Now for this Life, there comes some check, some hindrance. You understand me."

I bowed, and so far lied, if a lie can be expressed by a gesture. If the bow meant, however, that I wished she would gabble on, without requiring me to contribute to the conversation, it was a very true bow, and virtuous.

"There comes some hindrance, some difficulty. Unutterable, if you please; what is utterance? It is like—it is like the shimmer on the wheat when it rises to the sun in June. What is the shimmer? Is it more wind; is it less wind? I do not know. You do not know; no one knows. And this check comes on Life, if I must call it Life, this difficulty, this hindrance, and then you men send for a doctor and expect him to give belladonna, or castor oil; or the most sympathizing of you, you yourself, dear Mr. Mellen, talk of appetite or going to drive."

I was going to make some apology, when she went on:

"No, Mr. Mellen, when you have bathed in agony, as I have now for eight nights, you do not rise in the morning to fall to sweeping, and cooking, and writing letters, and receiving visits, and returning them, as if the machinery of life needed no oil. You talk of food——"

In fact, I had said no word of food.

"I do assure you, Mr. Mellen, that this bit of toast with the mushroom sauce upon it which I ate just now, unconsciously, while I was talking to you, is the only food that has passed my lips, without a struggle, since that fatal day of the athletics. Indeed, I might say it is all that I have eaten, excepting some boiled rice on Tuesday—no, Wednesday—and my regular Murdock's food at noon, which I force down, and my toast-water before going to bed. I take that toast-water from a superstition, but the pain is just the same."

All this went on in an undertone at our end of the table. The children beyond us were carrying on the thorough-going business of breakfast. Beyond them was John Fisher himself, joking with them, while Mrs. Grattan's seat and Miss Bell's were empty. For them to be late was unusual.

When they did come in, breakfast, for the rest of us, was nearly finished. Their morning dresses were so pretty, and their flowers so fresh, and both of them in such gay spirits, that John Fisher rallied them on their delay. He said they had some scheme of conquest before them, and that, like many a great general, they had taken so much time for preparation that they had lost the battle before it began. "The chickens are cold," he said; "the kidneys are eaten up, the coffee is cold, and, what is worse, by this time Mary is inevitably cross. She will send up word that there is not an egg in the house, that no coffee came from Ward's yesterday, and that we have had the last; she will say that she has just put coal upon the range, and that nothing can be heated. No, if you can satisfy yourself with a cracker, they say it is from Boston, Miss Mary, and a pickle, I think there is, you will do. Possibly we can find an olive."

Mary Bell laughed at her very prettiest; the sunniest laugh, it seemed to me, that ever passed over a lovely face. "It is Cordelia's fast-day, I believe, in her church. Is it not St. Anthony's day, or St. Barbara's day, Cordelia? I think Mr. Mellen has some crisp codfish by him. As for me, I spoke to Ellen Rideau as I came down-stairs. I told her that I should live with just an omelette, and some cream-toast, and a quail, if there was one, and some Indian cakes, if Mary would send up a chop and some buckwheats afterwards. Ellen is my friend, and here the omelette is."

In fact Ellen appeared with their breakfast at the moment.

"But all this does not explain," said John Fisher, "why you are both so late. Have you been out to church anywhere? We are so very catholic and cosmopolitan here

that I am always on the look-out for some new rite. Has
Dr. Witherspoon instituted morning vespers, or midnight
nones or trines, or anything else, by way of helping on his
canvass for alderman? And have you to be off every time
the third Monday before the second Tuesday after the seventh
Sunday after midsummer falls on a full moon?"

"Mr Fisher," said Cordelia, "you shall hold your peace.
I should think no one was ever down-stairs two seconds late
in this house before. If you will have the Amphions, and
John Caruthers, with his magnificent tenor, and the Chicago
quintette playing in the moonlight all night, what do you expect of two music-mad girls in the morning?"

"Amphions!" cried John Fisher, aghast.

"John Caruthers!" cried Mrs. Fisher.

And even the children stopped their chatter in amazement. The amazement was too evident for any one to sus-
pect acting. And it was Mrs. Grattan's turn to be amazed,
and Mary Bell's.

"Do you mean that you slept all through the serenade?"

"Serenade!" said John Fisher. "Do you tell me that
all these people have been on my lawn last night, and have
not had a bit of cheese or a biscuit?"

"Surely you heard them, Mrs. Fisher. I saw the light
in your room," said Mrs. Grattan.

"I heard them, Cordelia? How can you ask? You
know that just in those heavy hours of my first sleep I hear
nothing. It is a comatose state, I believe. I am dead, or
might be." And she went on with some details of the physi-
ology of sleep, which would have surprised Dr. Hammond.

But I am afraid no one listened.

" I am ashamed of you, John Fisher, " said Mrs. Grattan.
" And you, Mr Mellen. To be sure, your room is out of
the way. No; I am ashamed of myself, that I did not go
round the house with a watchman's rattle, which I brought
from Cincinnati with me. Or, really, we had better have a
gong. Mr. Fisher, you must have a gong to hang at the
door of my room, if you do mean to have the first musicians
in America come at night to play on your lawn."

"I do not care so much for the playing," said Fisher,
" as I do for the supper. Mary will kill me in the first
place ; or, if I escape her, I shall not dare look in the face
any cornet-à-piston for ten years. ' Page, squire and groom ;'
that there was no one my halls have nursed to give those
poor fellows a graham cracker, or a cup of water. Who
do you say was here, and what did they play?"

Then it appeared that, a little after midnight, the stillness
had been broken by an exquisite song by Caruthers, whose
perfect tenor, in those years, had no equal this side the
ocean, or the other. Then the Quintette Club, which was
passing through Tamworth on a visit, played something exquisite, but the ladies were not agreed what it was. By this
time, they had both been on the alert ; had their gas lighted,
and were in communication with each other. They had
agreed that it would be a shame to call Mrs. Fisher, if by
good fortune she were asleep. This was the form by which
they now expressed themselves. I suppose that in fact they
knew she would take it ill, whatever they did, and so that
they elected the simplest course.

" As for you, Cousin John, as the serenade was right in
front of your room, and so that, even if we had peeped out,

we could not have seen Mr. Caruthers, unless he came round
to look for us, and as the orchestra was at least twenty
pieces, we did not think that we must come and knock a
tattoo on your door. Another time we will."

"Another time!" groaned poor John Fisher. "Do you
think they will ever come this side of Clarion street? Not
a doughnut, or a piece of custard pie for them! They must
have been in a hurry. Were going over to some Turner
Hall, perhaps."

"Hurry? It was not what I call hurry. I looked at my
watch when I put on my wrapper and it was then half-past
twelve. When I got into bed again, the cuckoo was singing
two and a quarter. Why, Caruthers sang four or five times,
the Amphions sang that round they sang at the concert; they
sang Korner's battle-hymn; they sang that weird air James
wrote for the Alcestis. Oh, they sang, five, six—I do not
know how many times! Then the quintette people had always something between the choruses. Why, John, it was
a regular concert!"

"And I snoring in harmony," said he, lugubriously.
"And these fine fellows reduced to refreshing themselves
with lager, and cursing me for my stinginess. Well, I will
organize a night watch, if you girls stay any longer here, to
detect serenades. But then nobody will ever serenade this
house again."

And he turned to his newspaper for his consolation. The
older children began persecuting the ladies for details.
"How did Mr. Caruthers look? Did he stand up, or did
he sit on one of the piazza chairs?"

"My child, you do not suppose that I stood at the window throwing kisses to Mr. Caruthers, or that I peeped from behind a curtain. The utmost which we dared do was to light the gas. I opened Mary's door and found her lighting hers. Then we had to be very careful about the shadows. You have to have some shadows on a curtain in a serenade, but as the professor told us, at Vassar, they must be suggestive shadows, or indicative, and not too realistic. There must not be an exact profile of a night-cap, or of a disheveled head, but there must be something that indicates life and motion. Indeed, it should also indicate joy or enthusiasm, mingled with repose and a sense of refreshment. We practiced last night on the wall. Mary had a feather duster, and I had a warming-pan, which we tried effects with, but none of them succeeded. At last, however, Mary got some fine broad effects to move across the curtain by putting out her gas, and carrying a candle backward and forward behind a rocking-chair."

Mary Bell only laughed, as her reckless friend rattled on. To this moment, I believe there were some shadows, I know not what, manufactured for the occasion.

John Fisher roused from his newspaper.

"And all the hospitality this house could offer to thirty of the first artists in the country was a set of shadows on a curtain." Then he flung down his paper in scorn. But his eye rested on its title.

"Registered as second-class matter," he said. "I would give them a certificate that it was fifth-class matter, if they asked me, and low grade at that. If there were but one of them, I would send it to the museum as a curiosity; but so many, each more stupid than another, there is no room in any museum for them all. But there is one piece of news, Mary ; it will interest your friend Mr. Rossiter."

Why did her face flush crimson, just as I saw it that night in the gallery of the town hall, when the Dutchman was speaking. She tried to speak calmly.

" What has happened to Mr. Rossiter?"

" Oh, nothing has happened to him, strictly speaking. What I meant was that old Mr. Shearman is dead. He has been in Europe for his health, which means that he has been in Florence and Switzerland dying. He died day before yesterday, it seems. That means promotion in the Life office. Haggerston will be the president, all of them will be pushed up a peg, and Rossiter, who provides brains for the crowd, will have a decent salary, which he has been earning now for four or five years, without receiving it."

Mary Bell knew she must say something. " He certainly seems to work very hard." I do not think John Fisher observed that she spoke with special interest or difficulty. But I did. Fisher had done with his newspaper. Every one had finished breakfast. And as he rose he said, " I should think he did. Take him for all in all, Rossiter is one of the finest fellows who tread shoe-leather."

CHAPTER XXIV.

THE mystery, if I may call it so, of Mary Bell's crimson blush was revealed to me before night, and I learned some other things which, had I been wiser, or less conceited, I might have guessed at before.

I had vainly tried to gain a private interview with her. I did not mean to be foiled by Mrs. Fisher, as I had been once before, when I had thought that I could bring Miss Bell to say whether she cared for me more than for any other man, and whether she knew that life was very little to me, unless it were all knit in with the thought of her.

But Miss Bell was out almost all day to-day. Nor had there been any excuse by which I could attach myself to her goings or comings.

An hour before tea-time, as I was writing in my own room, the servant brought me a card. Mr. Rossiter was down-stairs and would like to see me.

What in the world did he want to see me for? If there was any one in the world whom I did not want to see it was Mr. Rossiter. I had even fondly wished that Mr. Fisher, with that same long arm of his, which had sent to Antwerp a candidate who stood in the way of reform, might take up George Rossiter and lift him to Yokohama, and establish him there permanently at the head of a Life company. More than once, when the carnal man was to much for me, had I felt willing to wring George Rossiter's neck and throw his head out of the window. Yet I knew he was an excellent fellow. I could even see he was a most agreeable man. If it had not been so, I should have liked him better ; strange to say, I had never got well over my surprise when Miss Bell sent for him on an exigency. Why could not I do as well as he?

What did Mr. Rossiter want of me now?

He was not in the parlors. The servant led me to what we called the small book-room.

Rossiter met me, a little pale, but with a smile which tried to be cordial. Still it was clear that he was high-strung, and that he was ill at ease.

"I asked them—I told them to show me here, because —yes, well—because I wanted to speak with you alone."

I happened to remember that only a few days before Mrs. Fisher sailed in on me in one of the elegant satin saloons, where I had never seen any one in the daytime before. I said, gravely, that we should be alone here unless Mrs. Fisher came in.

He smiled, with rather a sickly smile.

"Mr. Mellen," he said, "really you must pardon me. You will not understand my coming to you as I do. But I am strangely without friends here in Tamworth. In my own home, in Binghamton, I should have more than one person to turn to."

"Heavens!" I said to myself, "this fine young fellow is hard up, and wants to borrow money." Ah! if it had been that, I should have known what to say then.

He evidently spoke with difficulty; had found difficulty in bringing himself to speak. But he was resolute, and meant to put through what he had to say, difficulty or no.

"I asked for Miss Bell," he said, "but she is not in. Do you know where she is gone, or if she will be in soon?"

This was cool, to say the least, and it took me on a weak spot. But I did not mean to give myself away. I answered, with as little fierceness as possible, that I did not know. I conquered the temptation to say, "I thought you were the man who knew her plans; I do not interfere with them."

"It is foolish in me to ask," he said. "But drowning

men catch at straws. I want to see her. I want to see her to-day. And yet," he said after a pause, "I do not know that I ought to see her, and that is the reason why I made courage to send for you, Mr. Mellen. I say I made courage, for I certainly had none to spare."

I was amazed, and began to be curious. Nay, I had certain hopes. Had Mary Bell rejected his suit, and was he going to consult her or me as to whether he should cut his throat or drink laudanum?—I bowed, with that fatuous, benevolent look of a man who is complimented when his advice is asked, does not wonder that it is asked, and his bow and smile intimates that he will give advice, now it is asked, of the very first quality. Mr. Rossiter went on :

"It is absurd for me to suppose that you do not know— every one knows and may well know for all me—how entirely I admire Miss Bell. To you, Mr. Mellen, who are I know, my friend, it is almost a pleasure to say it aloud— to hear myself saying it—that she is the noblest woman and the dearest in the world, though she gives me no chance to say so to her, and though I do not know if she cares a straw for me."

There was this resemblance between Mr. Rossiter's position and mine that I could not but be half amused even while I was provoked, that he should bring me to this unusual and unnecessary confidence. Was every stripling who admired Mary Bell to come and tell me so? I should have my hands full. But I had no disposition to say this or anything unkind to him. Nay, the thought flashed across me, and for an instant it was rapture, that he had detected in his close watch of her that she prized some other man

more than she did him, and that, with a manliness which I
had heard of in romances, the fine fellow had come to say so.

Under this fleeting thought I listened to him with much
more interest.

" The truth is, Mr. Mellen, that I have had no right, till
to-day, to make any advances to Miss Bell. She has been
kind to me, she is kind to every one. But she treats me
—well—she treats me as she treats Mr. Fisher, or you, Mr.
Mellen, or any other gentleman whom she respects. Now,
to-day, I have a right to speak to her. Had I found her at
home, I should have known before now, and I should not
trouble you. But you are older than I—you know men
and women—you are not in love—— " And here he tried
to laugh, with that sickly failure that he made before.

" You will tell me, I think, fairly and kindly, whether
what I have to say to her is absurd." He gave me no chance
to answer. "Till to-day," he said, " I have been living
from week to week on a copying clerk's salary. If Mr.
Shearman came back, I might be discharged any instant,
if he wanted my place for a son or a nephew. To-day all
is changed. The directors offered me, an hour since, a fixed salary of fifteen hundred dollars. The moment the office
closed, I came to ask Miss Bell to share it with me, and to
be the joy and light of my life. Now, tell me, is this absurd? Have I any right to ask such a woman as that to
give me everything, when I can give her so little?"

Really, till that moment, I had thought, fool that I was:
first, that in an impulse of generosity the young man was going
to tell me that the field was, perhaps, mine; and when that
thought faded away, I had thought that he was going to ask

if it were mine, that he might be spared mortification. And it seemed that neither thought had crossed his mind!

Possibly it was I that was the fool, and not he.

I had to say something, such are the exigencies of conversation. And I did say, "What can I tell you? Why do you come to me?" I think he was too eager to see that I was cool.

"To you? I come to you because you are kind to me always; you are older and have experience; you see the game from the outside and you can tell. Mark you, I do not ask whether Miss Bell will accept me. That she must tell me herself. I want to know whether a poor clerk, with fifteen hundred a year, has any right to ask her. She is comfortable, she is happy. Is it an insult to ask her to leave a life of luxury such as Mr. Fisher gives her here, to share a life of work and—well, not privation, but economy, parsimony, if you please, like mine? You know the world. You know what men expect and women expect. Am I a fool to ask? Is it wrong to ask? When she was not here, I thought I might strengthen myself by asking you."

The poor dog had come to ask me, because I was an unprejudiced adviser! I was sitting serene on the heights above such follies, and could not be warped by any tenderness! Had it come to this? I looked round to see if there was a mirror, to find if he had rated me at seventy or at eighty. Once more I parried his eager question.

"Ask her by all means, if you feel as you do. You can put to her your own questions. Or Mrs. Grattan, might you not advise with her?"

"Mrs. Grattan! Do not play with me, Mr. Mellen.

You must understand me. When you asked your wife to
marry you, did you, could you say to her that, because you
loved her, you wanted her to share—well, as humble a life
as a man could well live in, with such means as I offer this
lady?"

" As to that," said I, rather grandly this time, " there is
no Mrs. Mellen, so that I cannot answer your question as
you put it. There never has been any. But this is certain,
my dear Mr. Rossiter. Women do not think of such things
as men do. Go and ask her yourself. That is her right ;
nay, it is yours. If Miss Bell loves you, she will marry you,
though your income be the dividend on two cents invested in
Arkansas bonds." His face beamed on me, as if it had
been the face of an angel. "If she do not love you, you
will find it out. She will not give you a hint of encourage-
ment, not if your salary be as much as Mr. Vanderbilt's
capital.

" No, dear Mr. Rossiter, it is a thing where no man can
advise, not even a man as old and as experienced as I."

Did he see that he had wounded me? Or was he so
eager in the hope of meeting her that the interview already
annoyed him, though he had brought it on?

I do not know. I only know that he rose, thanked me
cordially and went away.

And I was left to reflect, that all my delicate attentions to
Miss Bell had been so very delicate that an intelligent
young man, keen and quick to observe, had not so much as
noticed them ; that while I had hated him as a rival, almost
since I saw him, he had never dreamed that I was in the
race ; and to recollect that it had been squarely said to me

that I had passed too far along in the course of life, that I was not to be counted as interested in its passion. I had been distinctly told that I was henceforth not a participator but a judge or an adviser.

If he thought that, what would Miss Bell think and say? .

I could not read, after this. I could not write. After chafing over it for an hour, I determined to walk out, and take my chances of meeting her on her return.

I did meet her. But he had met her before me. They were talking together in the most animated way. But I could not catch his eye as they passed me.

CHAPTER XXV.

AND at last Tuesday came, the fatal Teusday which was to decide between THEM and US ; between cheap government and reckless waste : between a quiet town, minding its own business, and the rowdyism and recklessness and plunder of It.

Of course I had no vote, nor had little Stepney, who had spent the night with us, having come over to speak at the farewell mass meeting of the night before. But John Fisher drove us both down town, at eight in the morning, in the open wagon, which he was to use all day. He gave himself personally to the canvass, and we had all breakfasted early, that he might be at his precinct at the very beginning. The ladies, excepting Mrs. Fisher, who sent word that she had a bad headache, were with us. And before the day was over,

I found it was quite as busy a day with them, as with the
men.

At Fisher's precinct everything was quiet at that hour,
but the forces were gathering. On window-seats in the
corners of the room were already piles of "stickers,"—
separate ballots for individuals, with gum on the back that
they might at once be fastened over the printed names on
regular tickets. I saw bottles of mucilage, ready for similar
use, left by one or another Independent voter, who wanted
to facilitate Independency, and ran the risk of its telling
against his friends. The vote distributors of the several
parties were on perfectly good terms with each other; I
fancy, indeed, that in that precinct, IT had put forward its
best-appearing men, in the hopes to conciliate a few votes
from bolters who would not respect the final decisions of
"OUR" committee. There was no wrangling there, and
Fisher told me afterwards, that there was none all day.
Even at this early hour a hackney coach would arrive once
in every few minutes, from which descending a neatly-
dressed rallying man, with our colors, blue and white, in his
button-hole, would carefully lift out a lame man, or a man
with his face tied up in a handkerchief, once a man ac-
companied by two daughters, who, in quite dramatic fashion,
attended the invalid to the rail, where he dropped his vote.
Then the two Hebes looked scornfully at us men, as if to
say, " Why did you not let us vote in his place?" For
my part I did not know, and do not, why we had not sent a
man to his door, with a book in which he could register his
vote over his autograph signature.

Stepney and I staid long enough to see the mechanism of

the thing, which almost always differs a little in one state from another. As we walked away, we passed, what I had not noticed before, the Woman's Rallying Office. A little blue and white flag hung over the door with the invitation "Come in," and what was more certain, two bright girls on the door-step said, "Will you not have a cup of coffee?"

We both went in, and sure enough, there were a dozen little tables, with our ballots scattered over them, a vase of gentians and candy-tuft on each table, and at least half of them, men sitting, who had been lured in by these sirens, and, perhaps, by the memory of faultless coffee, served there in years before. Behind a counter at the end of the room, I saw several ladies whom I knew, among others Mrs. Grattan and Miss Bell. They were all dressed in uniform, with natty white caps and aprons, with rosettes of blue and white. "Pretty waiter-girls," from the very best ranks of Tamworth social order, were flying backward and forward and filling the cups of the men who were talking politics. Mrs. Tristum beckoned us to join a group of ladies who were sitting near the door.

"Have you come to help us, or are you only loafers?" said she. "If you will help, you shall have coffee, though you are but poor sticks anyway, both of you, seeing you had no more votes then women. But you shall each have one cup, in memory of last night's speeches. Mr. Stepney, you converted one man. I heard him say this morning, that that little fellow who told the war-story fixed him."

I asked what they were doing, and what they were expecting.

"My dear Mr. Mellen, we are at least showing our

colors, and that is one comfort. We are not chafing at home, and wondering how the battle goes. Then we have an eye on things here. There is not a young lawyer, nor a young doctor, nor a young engineer, nor a young dry-goods clerk in this ward who will forget to vote to-day. Some woman would say to him, the first time she met him, 'We might have lost the fourth ward by one vote, Mr. Smith; pray where were you?' So far we do something. What is more, is, that we do catch an undecided man sometimes, and we make him see that there can be a decent drinking-room without It; at least he sees that decent people are in earnest."

And she told me that I should find a rallying room like hers at any precinct; there were forty-four in all. They had done this, now for three years, and were sure good came of it. The men on duty told them so. In fact, before the day was over, I guessed that there were a good many more " men on duty" than there would be had there not been such comfortable quarters for them. " You can take your lunch here, you know," said Frank Heron to me about noon. But it did seem to me that he was more interested in that pretty Clara Orth, than he was in the lunch he was waiting for.

Things were by no means so Arcadian and elegant in other wards, Before the day was over, Stepney and I look-ed in upon almost every precinct; though we missed some, we were in every ward, and saw almost all the humorous, not to say passionate struggles of the day. It had its head-quarters, as well as We; and if whiskey and lager were paid for, it was certainly not by retail payment at these places. I could see here, however, that there was method in the madness which ruled there. More than once, when some drunken dog stepped up, with his most dignified air, to the man who dispensed one drink or another, his hopes were sharply, not to say profanely, crushed. "What business had he there, when he had neglected to register, or had never been naturalized?"

Free liquor was not for men without votes. It drew the line somewhere, and It drew it there. Indeed, I was amused to see how much care was exercised in such matters. It seemed as if there was fear that the supplies might give out.

In Boston, they used to let them have a keg of beer behind the voting-rail, for the use of the inspectors of votes, so that they might keep their sight clear to the end, and their faculties for counting. But this was not tolerated in the simpler conditions of Tamworth.

In three different wards, we saw a very pretty fête, as Jan Hooft, at the head of the wire-men, who made a regiment of nearly four hundred, came round, that the men might vote together. The regiment, if I may call it so, escorted in this manner its own members to the several precincts. I was told that they had men in eleven different precincts, and they went to all. These men, only the year before, had scattered their votes among all the candidates. But Jan's brilliant speech had made him a hero. Some injudicious thing said about Dutchmen, by a Norwegian orator, had closed up the ranks of the Sons of Holland, so that they voted as one man; and here were all the workmen from Kellert's establishment, and from the Coöperative, wearing blue gentians tied with white ribbon, and march-

ing with a band of music to vote our ticket in their respective wards. Salter had taken very little by his motion the
evening when he called Jan Hooft forward as a leader of
the people.

The women knew about what time this cohort would
appear in each ward. And they made special preparation for
its arrival. It was not to be expected that it should break
ranks so long that the men could take turns in drinking in-
doors. Indeed, I hope nobody expected that each of four
hundred men should drink forty-four cups of anything as
that day went round. But, with stronger force than that of
" pretty waiter-girls," they " policed " a part of their sidewalk, and had tubs of lemonade, and pails of coffee, ready
mixed with its milk and sugar, so that as the procession halted,
and the platoons for that place voted, the men in the others
stepped out and refreshed themselves. Perhaps cockades
or button-hole bouquets were pinned on at the same time, by
canvassers, in defiance of civil service regulations. Jan
Hooft himself, before the day was over, was one moving
mass of white and blue.

Once and again, as the day went by, we met John Fisher
himself, as he brought to the polls some man of lonely work,
who would hardly have left his little office or his lonely
store, and locked the door, to sacrifice to his country the
chance of the customer who might come in his absence of
half an hour.

But it was quite a different thing when John Fisher
came round to his place cheerily : " How is business, Mr.
Broadcloth?" or, "All right, Dr. Molar ; I have brought
you my friend Mr. Titus, who will stay, and see that nobody

steals anything, till we come back. We will soon get you to the polls." Indeed, neither Mr. Broadcloth nor Dr. Molar was displeased to have a chance to drive behind John Fisher's bays, and to discuss the political chances with him. On his part, he was as well pleased to test in a day the real feeling of the bone and sinew of the community which he was trying to serve.

There had been no announcement at breakfast of any hour for lunch at home. It seemed to be expected that we should find our meat and drink where we did our work. And that day no one in our little circle affected to attend to anything but this election. Fisher told me that his works were open, and the engines running all day. "But then," he said, "every man is allowed four hours for voting, and they are as much excited about it—well, as I am ; so that we shall not show a great deal of ' subduing brute matter,' as I think you call it, in to-day's work there. The brute matter we shall subdue to-day is somewhere else."

The day was fine, and there was no pretence that bad weather kept any one at home. As sundown drew near, lugubrious peals on the church bells summoned any laggards, as if to a funeral. But there were but few laggards. I happened to be, however, at a precinct which was just opposite the Grand Junction station of the Cattaraugus and Opelousas Road, when this tolling began. An instant more and I heard cheering, and, with Stepney, I ran out from Miss Water's comfortable head-quarters to see what was passing. An engine, without baggage car, and with only one passenger car attached, engine and car both festooned with blue and white, dashed in, amid the cheers of fifty people. Some twenty young men, wearing our colors, jumped out. They had engaged this special car to bring them from Chicago, so that they might arrive two hours before the regular train, and a few minutes before the polls closed. A dozen wagons were waiting to take them to their precincts. Much opening and shutting of watches made it clear that, even at number three in Ward VII, they would be in time. They all dashed off amid the cheers of admiring loafers, the crowd melted away, and the station was left as dull and stupid as it usually was.

Stepney and I waited to see the votes counted, and sealed, and to hear the public proclamation made in that precinct. When the messenger was dispatched to the central precinct in that ward, we walked across to Ward IV where we had begun the day. Fisher was waiting for us. " There is no good of staying here any longer," he said; " we shall know the news at home sooner than we shall here." I saw he was disturbed, in a moment. For me, I had been made thoroughly cheerful by the activity of the day, and, in my optimistic way, I had taken for granted that so much good work on the right side could not have been done in vain. As we rode home I sounded him. But he could not well tell why he was anxious. In that ward all was well. But they had known it would be. It had done better, for that matter, than their canvass promised. All the high and dry people, who would not help in the canvass at all, because they were so bigoted about purity of elections, and who would not commit themselves in advance, lest on the morning of the election, some angel from heaven should tell them that drunkenness and lying and stealing were cardinal virtues, all these people had, at the last, voted with "Us," so that the returns looked better than our canvassers dared to predict. "But this was no evidence, not the least," he said, "for the out-lying wards." Whether he had private advice of which he would not speak, or whether this was the depression which comes over a strong man, because he cannot be everywhere, I could not guess. But it affected us all three. And, after a little effort, we drove home in silence.

CHAPTER XXVI.

But, as we turned into the avenue, with the change of scene our spirits rose at once.

Mrs. Fisher, and Cordelia Grattan, and Miss Bell, were all on the portico, waving handkerchiefs. The flag had been flying on the top of the house all day. But a smaller flag was now twined in, somehow, with the vines on the trellis. And, as we came near enough to hear, Mary Bell cried, "Victory! Victory!" We did not know what they were cheering about. But, as John Fisher threw his reins to the groom, she gave him a despatch. "All is, we have carried the Bloody Third," she cried, "and you owe it to the women!"

"Carried the Third?" said John Fisher with scorn. "Give us news that we can believe for a second, at least."

"Read, read, read! incredulous man! Read it on the housetops." And he read aloud:

"I hope that I am the first to tell you that we have carried the Third by seven votes. They could not stand against the women, to whom we owe nineteen votes at least. I will come up and tell you when the votes are sealed.   GEORGE ROSSITER."

"Who is this to?" said John Fisher.

"It is to me," said Mary Bell, proudly enough, though perhaps provoked a little, both with herself and with him, that he had forced the avowal. But the joy of the moment was something behind and beyond all personal annoyances.

"Carried the Third!" repeated Fisher, almost as if he talked to himself. "Miracles are beginning! I should as soon—and Rossiter must be right. He is an inspector there, with two of these hounds against him. They would have died hard. But Rossiter is never fooled. Carried the Third, indeed!"

And he ran in, to his own telephone-box.

"Hello! Give me 219." Then, after a pause:

"Who is there?" And again:

"Ask Frank if he knows we have carried the Third." And after Frank's reply, inaudible to us, he continued:

"It *is* impossible, but all the same we have done it. We have seven majority." Another pause, while he listened, and then he said——

"No; there is no possible mistake. Rossiter is there, and we have this from him."

In an instant this miracle had changed the man. "I hope you asked your friend to dine, Mary. The man who sends us such news ought to be crowned with laurels."

And when she said that she had done no such thing, he sent a servant to the public telephone with a message to Mr. Rossiter that he must come up as soon as they could spare him. He would not use his own wire for anything but to receive news.

Such was the beginning of three hours of intense anxiety, and curiosity, hope rising and hope deferred and hope prostrated under foot, fear and surprise alternating, such as cannot be forgotten, but as I cannot pretend to describe. By common consent, we gathered in his own den, where was the telephone wire. When the oracle spoke he was almost always the Python, if one may say so, who did what Pythonesses should do when oracles are speaking. But sometimes he deputed Mary Bell, if, as would happen, he was writing or calculating, when the telephone bell rang.

The first news was a set of black reactions from Rossiter's jubilant despatch. Mrs. Edwards had furnished late afternoon tea, and we were still discussing the possible causes of our success in the Bloody Third, when from precinct something in the Fifth comes this dark omen :

" We are nineteen behind our canvass. They are seventy-two ahead of theirs. No one knows why."

" Can you give us the figures?" Fisher replied.

" Two ninety-seven ; five thirty-one ; nineteen scattering."

There seemed to be no necessity to tell for whom these numbers had voted. Nor was there. Fisher wrote them on the blank sheet he had ready ruled for the forty-four precincts.

"Bad enough," he said to us. "For the other precincts will do worse. And this was at best but a doubtful ward." And then, with his tea, again he tried to explain to Mrs. Grattan what was the matter there, when the bell struck again.

"Worse and worse," he said, after he had listened. "We shall lose another hundred in the Slab Bridge precinct. That means we lose the Fifth ward." And he sat down again to his cooler tea, and again tried to explain.

Mary Bell put down the figures on the sheet, and asked: "Perhaps their first precinct will do better. May I not ask?"

"Ask? Oh, no! It would only bother them. Hartshorn is there; he will tell as soon as he has anything to tell. He is making them count again, because things look so badly. He has heard from two, and three, and four. Four is of no great account, anyway."

As it happened, precinct four spoke at that moment. And, as before, he repeated the figures. She wrote them from his lips. "Two hundred ninety-one; three hundred seventy-four; twenty-one scattering."

"Twenty-one fools in that precinct and only nineteen in William's. How do you account for that, Mary?" This was Fisher's grim comment. She asked what she should put down for Slab Bridge. "Oh, nothing, nothing, till you have the exact numbers! These guesses are nothing."

Then he explained to me and to Stepney, seeing that we were strangely new to all this, that of course we generally received the news from the small precincts first, because those are most easily counted. This is the reason why the first news of our elections is so often undecisive, or, as an ignorant public supposes, not confirmed afterwards. The news is true enough. But the small precincts, of which the vote can be counted most quickly, though they are first reported, are not usually those which decide things.

"Not but that a small precinct may be the last to come in. They may have a bad counting-board, and one man may make things come out 211, and another 1102, and so you may have to begin all over again. If you have a drunken inspector, or a man who likes to quarrel, you may be all night before the votes are counted and sealed.

" We hold to the old New England traditions," he said, " and we count the votes in ' open meeting,' where any one can see. Of course we take care that, in each precinct. three or four men, who do not drink or steal or lie, shall be looking on."

At this moment a cab rolled up to the door, and George Rossiter joined us. Till this moment I had permitted myself to doubt as to the issue of his walk and talk the last night with Miss Bell. But from this moment I knew. Not that she stepped forward. No. She stepped back. Not that he sought her even with his eye. But that his face and air were of glad, calm certainty. He need not seek her. She was his, without more seeking. I dared to look at her. Again her face was crimson. But her smile of welcome was of absolute pride and joy.

" Where are the laurels for the hero?" This was John Fisher's welcome. And he gave the hero both hands.

" I do not see why I should be called the hero. I

only bring the good news. The heroes are Mr. Stepney, who makes the converts ; Mr. Mellen who meets the enemy, and you, Mr. Fisher, who direct the campaign."

" As to that," said poor John Fisher, ruefully, " I feel like a general in the war, when the scattered fire tells him that his right is lost in the fog, and his left has given way. Your ' Bloody Third ' is all very fine, and we thank you for your news. But what if we lost the Fifth ? "

" Lose the Fifth ! " cried Rossiter. " Impossible ! As well tell me that you have lost the Hill."

Then Mr. Fisher made him look at the fatal figures. And, at this moment, the telephone bell rang, and other figures, which seemed even worse, came from other pre-cincts. George Rossiter entered these, very silent, on the sheet prepared. He looked pale with distress and surprise.

"And we hear of nothing from our friends," said Mrs. Grattan, because she wanted to say something.

" No need to hear from them. Of some things we are sure, or ought to be. As sure as I was of the Hill an hour ago, when I was blue enough, while we were rid-ing home, Mellen." This was Fisher's grim and melan-choly answer. " What is it, Bruce ? Is Mrs. Edwards dead, or has the kitchen burned down ? Bad news comes at once."

Bruce smiled respectfully, and announced dinner.

" Dinner ? It is an hour too early." But no ; dinner had come, as it generally will come.

" We will wait on ourselves, Bruce. Stay here and call me when the bell rings."

So we went in to dinner. And literally, before dinner was over, Fisher or Rossiter ran to seventeen calls, as so many different precincts announced the totals which were proclaimed successively. The reader should understand that when this proclamation had been made " in open meeting," a certified copy of it, with the parcels of votes sealed carefully, were sent to the ward-room of the ward, where the respective ward officers prepared the full statement of the result. Sometimes there were three precincts in a ward, sometimes four, and sometimes even five.

But till dinner was over, though we had twenty-nine precincts of the forty-four returned, we could only make up two ward returns. And these, oddly enough, reversed exactly the definite canvass on which we had placed so much reliance. We had gained the " Bloody Third," which nobody expected to gain. But we had certainly lost the First, which we carried a year before, and had a fair chance of carrying now. The breweries had been too much for us.

"They naturalized two hundred men there since August," said Fisher, " and there has been free lager and free whisky on tap for a fortnight."

Actually at half-past eight o'clock, when we left the dinner table, where we had spent much more time in calculating than in dining, we were more in doubt than we were when we breakfasted that morning. And this, although we knew the result in two-thirds of the city.

" It is just the other third which we do not know," said John Fisher, ruefully.

We gathered, almost of course, in the telephone room

again, as if there were any satisfaction in being a few inches nearer to the whispers which sealed our fate. We had scarcely entered, when the bell rang. Fisher put his ear to the voice.

"It is Harkness," he said, laughing. And then his face kept the smile as it listened. He put his mouth to the tube and said, "Good for the loyal Seventh! Such figures were never heard of! My love and congratulations to Dr. Witherspoon, and to yourself, my dear boy." Then he listened, and in reply said, "We cannot tell, but you have done your part. Good-by."

"Such figures were never heard of," he said again, as he turned to the paper and put them down, taking Harkness's full return, and caring no longer for the votes of separate precincts. "We" had 2897, and "They" had only 674. "See, Mellen, one ward giving thirty-six hundred votes, when the whole city will not give thirty thousand. There is a gerrymander for you. Because the pirates know we could poll four to their one there. Thirty-six hundred and ninety votes in all. And they have not in the ward thirty-eight hundred on their register. That is what happens when Col. Stothers is willing to soil his gloves, and Dr. Witherspoon to stand as alderman."

And at this moment we heard a carriage drive up at the door. No one rang. The door flew open, and Mr. Jackson rushed in, unannounced. I had seen him at the house at more than one gathering.

"Have you heard—do you know? I asked Williams to let me bring the news. That is why he did not speak."

"We have heard a great deal," said Fisher. "Some things we did not want to hear."

" We have the Fifth after all! Sixteen clear majority over everything! They were sure of it, and we gave it up, after Slab Bridge caved in so awfully. But your Dutch friends, Mrs. Fisher, came up magnificently in that little precinct by Ofterdom's brewery. That precinct gave us three hundred square, where we expected less than nothing, and the Fifth is clean ours, aldermen, pig-wardens, school-committee, and all. Mrs. Fisher, the victory is yours."

Poor Mrs. Fisher was of all colors; so was John Fisher. Mary Bell was blazing red, and Cordelia Grattan was ashy pale. Mrs. Fisher only said:

" No, no; I did what I could. But I am only a woman. And I speak German so ill."

But by this time even the taciturn Jackson, now so voluble, had forgotten her. He was beside himself in his account of the revulsion of feeling at the ward-room.

" We waited, and we waited, blue enough, I can tell you. You know how bad it was in Slab Bridge, and number four was as bad."

" That was the first vote I had," said Fisher.

" The first any of us had. And we had all the large precincts. Each worse than the other, for I see you have them here. Square one hundred and ninety against us, and Ofterdom's to come in. And the fellows from there knew nothing. The whole day had been quiet, and these Dutchmen you see are not wire-men. They are in the leather shops, and no one seems to have known. Why, when the count was over—there, look at it: 464 to 159. Where we expected nothing and worse;—why the fellows on the spot did not believe it. They would not believe

it. They re-counted three times, and they would be counting now, but your hero, Mrs. Fisher, Jan Hooft, came in
with his band, and he swore he would hang them if they
did not make up the return and seal the votes. And they
could not help it, for four times it had come out the same
way. The figures are burned into my brain, 464 to 159.

"When that came up to us, with twenty people to
explain, was not the laugh on the other side? See our
totals, Mr. Fisher. We have one thousand and sixty-three.
They have nine hundred and forty-five and there are one
hundred and two scattering. You cannot be everywhere,
Mr. Fisher, but you should have been in our ward-room."

And this was the beginning of victory. All the time,
now, the telephone bell was ringing, or the door-bell.
Rossiter or Fisher or Miss Bell were listening at the telephone, or one or other of us was receiving eager canvassers,
who knew they should be welcome. Often, indeed, their
news had come before them, but no one was so cruel as to
tell them that. Before half-past nine, the whole house was
sure of the result. Every maid had blue and white ribbons
pinned on her pretty dress, and was dressed as for
company. All the men had fresh gentians, tied with white
satin in their button-holes. Every face was smiling. Bruce
and Barnard, with the Fisher boys and girls assisting, were
putting candles in the windows, and by ten o'clock the
whole front of the house was illuminated. I found they had
all the facilities for this in readiness. The large dining-
room was lighted, and wagons began to drive up from
the confectioners and caterers, who had been suddenly summoned by wire to send up stores for an impromptu feast
for which even Mrs. Edwards was not ready.

" He would have been very angry," she said to me in an aside, " if I had made the ices when I was not sure."

And people poured in so fast that I could see that all such preparations would not be amiss.

Briefly, we had carried nine wards out of twelve. Some we had swept cleanly, as we were meant to do when the town was districted. Some we had carried by a hair's breadth, as the " Bloody Third," and this fickle Fifth. Even one of the enemy's wards had broken on the aldermen and school-committee, and we had saved good Father O'Reilly, who had been put off their ticket by an infernal conspiracy, as Jackson told me. The victory was complete. Our mayor, who last year only squeezed in by a thousand or so, when the brewery was divided, had a fair majority of five thousand over everything. But this was little, if his hands had been tied. Instead of that, we had the best school-committee we had chosen for years, we had nine out of twelve aldermen, with councilmen in a proportion even larger. One by one, ladies from the neighborhood dropped in. One by one, all the gentlemen I had met at the meetings for consultation dropped in. There had gathered a party of a hundred of the most cheerful people in the world, when a band of music was heard and we all went out upon the large piazza to welcome a delegation. Fisher and the ladies of the house, with the children, stood together in the portico.

It was the same procession of the wire-workers which we had seen in the morning at the polling places. But, to-night, in a barouche close following the band of music, sat the newly-elected mayor, the president of the Amphions,

Jan Hooft and Jan Hooft's daughter, the child whose sing
ing had so delighted me at the school anniversary. The
band passed the portico, halted and continued playing till
they had come quite to the end of the Lohengrin wedding
march, which they played magnificently. A policeman of
immense grandeur, who felt the full importance of his
position, flung open the door of the carriage, and then
waited till the music was finished.

Then the mayor stepped out, handed out Jan Hooft and
the little girl, and Mr. Beekman followed them.

Fisher stepped forward and shook hands with all.

The mayor said but a word: "Mr. Fisher, we owe this
victory, first to Mr. Jan Hooft, and next to you. It is
with pleasure that I see you two join your hands. In such
a union Tamworth is safe." Turning to the crowd, he
cried, " Three cheers for Jan Hooft and John Fisher ! "

And band and crowd cheered with a will.

Jan Hooft almost crushed Fisher's hand in his eager grasp.

" Herr Fisher," he said, and he stopped. " Herr
Fisher," and he stopped again. " Herr Fisher, Dutchmen
be poor, but they know they friends. They be honest, Herr
Fisher. They hate lies, Herr Fisher. I have come mit
my daughter, mit all dem people, to dank Madame Fisher
for all she am done for dem Dutchmen, when dey was sick
and poor, Herr Fisher."

And he looked round, wistfully. He looked at Mrs.
Fisher with surprise. Then he saw Mary Bell, cowering
behind that lady.

" I see her," he cried gladly ; " she shall not be hided.
Come, come, come, Elspeth."

And the child by this time caught his wish, rushed forward between Mr. Fisher and Mrs. Fisher, and hid herself, as she had done on the day of the school celebration, in Mary Bell's arms.

In a moment more, she remembered that she was to give the magnificent bouquet she brought to her benefactress. She did so.

"She be one little girl, Mrs. Fisher," said Jan Hooft to Mary Bell. "She cannot say notting, she be so happy. But all de Dutch women in the town, Frau Fisher, know who be de friend who saved me, wen dat hund had me under he foot, Frau Fisher, and de Dutch men, who be poor, Frau Fisher, but be honest, and de Dutch women, Frau Fisher, dey send you dem flowers, Frau Fisher, mit deir love, Frau Fisher, und deir danke."

John Fisher recovered himself in this long speech. Mary Bell kissed the child, and led her into the house.

Fisher stepped forward and cried, "Three cheers for Jan Hooft and all honest men!" and the crowd cheered lustily.

"Now come in, men," he said more colloquially. "Come in! Come in! Have something to eat. We have no lager, Walter," he said to one of them, "but I believe there is cold water."

And the crowd passed in. Not one person in a hundred knew what had passed, or understood the incident.

From that time till midnight, we were shaking hands, congratulating, welcoming and being welcomed. Every man who had a right arm was carrying out pails of coffee, and lemonade, and drinks without a name, but without spirit, upon the piazza.

"Have you forgiven me, Beckman, that I slept so sound-ly the night you serenaded us, or was it the ladies you serenaded? They heard you, as I think you know." This was John Fisher's apology to the Amphions.

And Beckman intimated, with a laugh, that in the joy of the victory, all was forgiven and forgotten.

CHAPTER XXVII, AND LAST.

I SLEPT wretchedly that night. Were it not that I remember, too well, Mrs. Fisher's exaggerations, in speaking of such matters, I should say that I did not sleep at all.

Was it that I had drunk too often, from the fragrant Mocha, at the forty-four Ladies' Rallying Rooms which I had visit-ed? Or had I forgotten my own rules, when tempted in the evening, by Mrs. Edwards' handiwork, at our own house?

Was the victory such a marvel that I must lie awake all night to think over the details?

Or, alas, was it that, to my careful watchfulness, the triumphant evening left no longer one quiver of uncertain hope as to Miss Bell's likes or dislikes among her admirers?

Or, alas, again; was it this mystery which connected her so certainly with the affair of the necklace? Was she capable of pawning a tinsel gewgaw for money, even if she had the excuse that she was to use the money for the noblest purpose? And had she not willingly left me in the notion which she knew I had, as Jan Hooft had, that it was Mrs. Fisher had done that bad thing?

All together, I did not sleep, or I did not think I did. Had there been a serenade that night, I should surely have been the first to know it.

And I was, naturally enough, the first in the breakfast-room.

But John Fisher joined me soon. He was radiant.

" Surely life is worth living," he said, " when things can be done so cleanly and thoroughly. How can anybody doubt of the people, if you only make the people to care for itself?'

I stammered out some congratulation. He really did not observe that I was so dull.

" I am used to surprises," he said. " The unexpected is what happens. But not the unexpected all along the line. Our ladies are late," he said, "and as for the children, I would not have them called. Once a year, and after a glorious victory, they may sleep over."

At that moment one of the maids came in to say that Mrs. Grattan was in the conservatory and sent word that she would be in, in a few minutes, when Donald had given her some more roses.

" Mrs. Fisher will not be down," he said, "but where is Miss Bell?" The girl smiled, and said she saw Miss Bell go out in the garden.

"Oh, then it is all right," said Fisher, laughing. " Rossiter breakfasts with us and they will be in by the time the coffee is cold." And he rang for breakfast.

We were alone together, and I might as well make him solve my mysteries.

" Mr. Rossiter and Miss Bell understand each other very well," I said, doubtfully.

" I do not see why there should be any mystery to you,"

he said. " I am not at liberty to say anything. But I cannot help your guessing what you choose. He is a fine fellow and she is a queen among women. Nothing could be better—if they choose to engage themselves," he added, as if to save himself from telling anything.

" Yet I cannot understand," blundered I. " You would not have thought, that even for such a purpose, she would have pawned a necklace."

" Mary Bell pawn the necklace!" Poor Fisher looked as if I had struck him. " She never saw the necklace. Yet but for her, it would have ruined us all."

" She certainly used the money," I said coolly. " She certainly paid Jan Hooft's debts."

"And why should she not pay his debts if she choose to? Miss Bell's fortune is three millions, if it is a cent. Her charities are not of the advertised kind, but no woman in America handles money more freely and more wisely. Is it possible you did not know this before?"

I said no, and the reader knows that this was so. I said that something he said to me in the mill had taught me that Mrs. Grattan was a rich woman, but I had supposed that his niece, if Miss Bell were his niece—she often called him Uncle John,—owed her home to his kindness, and to the same kindness owed her freedom from daily toil and from anxiety.

John Fisher looked at me with amazement as I said all this, and then said very frankly :

" That looks well for her—and for you," he added, after a pause.

" I am not the only person so deceived," I said.   " Mr.

Rossiter took my advice on Monday, as to whether, with fifteen hundred dollars a year, he could make a home which should be fit for her."

" Did Rossiter ask that? By Jove ! I like him better than ever. Hush ! Here they are."

Here they were. She came in radiant with beauty and happiness.

George Rossiter was radiant with manly pride. They held each other's hands for one moment in the hall. Then she turned abruptly to me.

"Mr. Mellen, we need have no secrets from you. You have been our true friend, and we know you will be."

At this moment, Cordelia Grattan pinned a bunch of exquisite roses in the breast of her dress.

And I was able, in a blundering way, to say I knew their life would be very happy.

THE END.

www.ingramcontent.com/pod-product-compliance
Lightning Source LLC
Chambersburg PA
CBHW030547040726
47497CB00008B/2606